The Dungeon of Doom

The Dungeon of Doom

John R. Erickson

Illustrations by Gerald L. Holmes

Puffin Books

PUFFIN BOOKS
Published by Penguin Group
Penguin Young Readers Group,
345 Hudson Street, New York, New York 10014, U.S.A.
Penguin Books Ltd,
80 Strand, London WC2R ORL, England
Penguin Books Australia Ltd, 250 Camberwell Road,
Camberwell, Victoria 3124, Australia
Penguin Books Canada Ltd,
10 Alcorn Avenue, Toronto, Ontario, Canada M4V 3B2
Penguin Books (N.Z.) Ltd,
182-190 Wairau Road, Auckland 10, New Zealand

Published simultaneously by Viking and Puffin Books,
divisions of Penguin Young Readers Group, 2004

5 7 9 10 8 6 4

ISBN: 0-14-240134-X

Hank the Cowdog® is a registered trademark of John R. Erickson.

Printed in the United States of America

For Gary and Kim

CONTENTS

CHAPTER ONE

Drover Tries to Scramble My Brains

It's me again, Hank the Cowdog. Why would anyone send the Head of Ranch Security to Obedience School? It beats me, and let me go on the record as saying that it was one of the dumbest decisions ever made on this ranch.

On any ranch. In the whole world.

Just think about it. After a dog has climbed the ladder of success and achieved the position of Head of Ranch Security, does he need to go back to Doggie Kindergarten? No sir. He needs to be turned loose and left alone so that he can hunt down the various monsters, spies, enemy agents, and crinimal villains who lurk in the darkness and plot evil schemes against the ranch.

Oh, and he needs to be working day and night

to humble the local cat. That's a huge point right there. If the Head of Ranch Security isn't around to humble the cats, who's going to do it? Nobody. And then you know what happens? The cats try to take over the ranch and run the whole show, and before you know it, the place has gone straight to pot.

You know who needs to go to Obedience School? CATS. They never take orders, and if you don't believe me, just hunt up the nearest cat and tell him to sit down. Ha. He'll give you one of those arrogant smirks and walk away with his tail stuck straight up in the air.

That's a cat for you, arrogant and selfish to the bitter end, but does anyone ever talk about sending cats to Obedience School?

Sorry for the outburst, but this thing really has me worked up. Actually, you're not supposed to know about the Obedience School yet. It comes later in the story. See, every story is composed of two parts: the First Part and the Second Part. If you knew what was coming in the Second Part, you might not read the First Part, and that wouldn't be good. First Parts should always come first and Second Parts should always . . .

Maybe this is obvious, so let's move on.

It began, as I recall, on a normal average day

on the ranch. Wait. It wasn't exactly a normal day. It was a roundup-and-branding day in the spring of the year, which means that it wasn't normal at all. It was one of the biggest workdays of the year.

Yes, it's all coming back to me now. I knew something was cooking when, at first light, I heard the sounds of unauthorized vehicles approaching ranch headquarters. After a long night of patrol work, Drover and I had just returned to the Security Division's Vast Office Complex beneath the gas tanks, and were in the process of fluffing up our stinking gunnysack beds.

You know why our gunnysacks smelled bad? Because the cowboys on this outfit were too cheap to buy us new ones. You can buy those gunnysacks at the feed store for fifteen cents apiece, and would it break the ranch's bank if they gave us fresh bed linens every six months or so? Heck no, but they don't. Those guys are so cheap, they'd skin a flea for the hide and tallow, but we can't get started on all the injustices in life.

The point is that we were fluffing up our beds, and yes, they smelled pretty rank. Just as I had completed the Three Turns Around the Bed Maneuver and was about to collapse into the loving embrace of my gunnysack, my Left Earatory

Scanner leaped up and began pulling in mysterious signals from the vaposphere.

Your ordinary mutts call them "ears." We call them Earatory Scanners because . . . well, they're quite a bit more sofissicated . . . suffiticated . . . saffistocated . . . phooey . . . quite a bit more impressive than ears. They're very sensitive scanning devices that can snag the tiniest of sounds out of the air—or the "vaposphere," to use our technical word for the air around us.

Anyway, my Left Earatory Scanner had soforthed and was so-forthing the whatever, and suddenly a red light began flashing on the control panel of my mind. I turned to my assistant.

"Drover, I don't want to alarm you, but I just received an alarm from Data Control."

"No thanks, I'm stuffed."

"Come back on that?"

"Murgle skiffer alarm blossom snicklefritz."

I narrowed my eyes and studied the runt. He was stretched out on his bed and appeared to be half-asleep. "Drover, I'm sounding General Quarters. Report to the bridge at once."

He sat up and pried open his eyes, revealing . . . well, not much, two empty holes. Those holes stared at me for a long moment before he spoke. "Oh hi. Was someone talking to me?"

"Affirmative. We have a problem."

"Oh drat, I hate problems." He struggled to his feet, swayed back and forth, and yawned. "You know, I just had the weirdest dream."

"I'm not interested in your dreams."

"Thanks. Yeah, there was this important general who'd built a bridge across troubled waters. And he was standing on the bridge . . . with an alarm clock."

"Was his name General Quarters?"

"That's the one. What was he doing with that clock?"

"Drover, listen carefully. I issued an alarm, not an alarm clock. I sounded General Quarters and ordered you to report to the bridge at once."

He glanced around. "I'll be derned. Where's the bridge?"

"The bridge is here, where the captain stays."

"No, I think he was a general."

"Drover, I am the captain of this ship and I have issued an order."

"You mean . . . we're on a ship? I hate water. It's always so wet. And I get seasick. Help! I want to go home!"

I caught him just before he dived under his gunnysack. "Drover, forget the bridge and skip the ship."

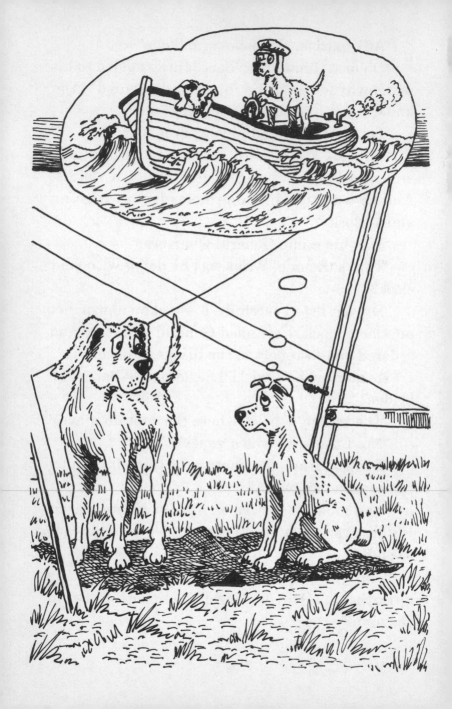

"Yeah, but I can't swim. Help! We're sinking!" He blinked his eyes and looked around. "Wait a second. We're not on a ship."

"Of course we're not, you goofball, and I never said we were. You know the trouble with you?"

"I hate water?"

"No."

"I can't swim?"

"No. Hush and I'll tell you. The trouble with you is that you take a perfectly good idea and run it into the ground."

"I did that?"

"Yes, you did. I tried to add a little color to the boring routine of waking you up, and ... never mind."

"You mean ... you mean we really *are* on a ship?"

Suddenly I felt that I was being crushed by the forces of chaos. I stumbled toward my bed and collapsed. "Just drop it. I can't stand any more of this. I've forgotten the point of this conversation and I no longer care. Go away and leave me alone."

"Well, okay. Nighty night."

"Nighty shut up."

There was a moment of silence, then ..."Hank, you know what? A pickup just pulled into headquarters. It's pulling a stock trailer and there's a horse in the back. Reckon we ought to bark the alarm?"

Huh?

I came ripping out of a deep . . . out of a shallow sleep, let us say. I mean, listening to Drover yap was enough to put anyone to sleep and, okay, maybe I had drifted off. But I came flying out of bed and took control of the situation.

"That's what I was trying to tell you, bug brain! Bark the alarm and prepare to launch all dogs! We've got trespassers on the ranch!"

And with that, we left sleep and comfort behind us, and went swooping up to the house to reconoodle a situation that was already looking pretty serious.

CHAPTER TWO

I Get Fired

You see what I have to go through with Drover?
I had received the alarm from Data Control
and was trying to call him into action, using some
new and interesting terminology from naval life,
and he... I don't know what he did or how he did
it, but this happens all the time. He gets me so
twisted around, I find myself... well, blabbing
nonsense.

You heard the whole thing, so you know what
I'm talking about. Sometimes I think the little
moron is trying to make a mockery of my life.

Oh well.

The important thing is that I managed to
sneeze control of the situation and get things moving in the right direction. We launched ourselves

into the morning breeze and went streaking north-eastward on a compass heading of 3400. Once air-borne, I gave the order to start sending out some Stage One Barkings, just to let the enemy know that we were . . .

Yipes. The pickup came barreling down the hill, heading straight toward us on a collision course, so I sent out an urgent message to begin Evasive Action. In a flash, we throttled down and leaped out of the roadway, just in time to . . . cough . . . eat dirt kicked up by the tires of the smarty-pants pickup.

Hey, who and where did that guy think he was? For his information . . . holy smokes, no sooner had the first pickup rumbled past than another appeared right behind it, and then another. And another. What was going on around here? It was just barely daylight, so what were all these people doing on my . . .

Okay, relax. You thought it was some kind of invasion of the ranch? Ha ha. Not at all. No, it turned out to be . . . have I ever mentioned that it's hard for a dog to do a proper job of running his ranch when nobody tells him what's going on? Well, it's not only hard, it's impossible.

Here's the deal. Slim and Loper, the cowboys on this outfit, had set up a branding day. They'd called all the ranchers and cowboys in the neighborhood to come and help with the work. So far, so good. I have no problem letting those guys play a small role in planning things around here. Give 'em a few little jobs to keep 'em busy and they'll stay out of my hair. But this!

See, they'd planned the whole day's work, they'd called everybody on the creek, BUT NOBODY HAD BOTHERED TO CLEAR IT WITH ME. So all at once we had all these unauthorized pickups pulling into ranch headquarters at daylight, and there I was . . . well, running around and barking like an idiot. How do you suppose that made me feel?

It made me feel pretty silly, is how it made me feel. Obviously we'd had a major breakdown in communications somewhere along the chain of command. Obviously someone on our ranch didn't think it was important to let the Head of Ranch Security know what was going on.

As the pickups rolled into headquarters one after another, I marched over to where Drover was standing. "This is outrageous. They expect us to protect the ranch and keep records on everyone who comes and goes, but then they cut us out of the loop."

He glanced around. "What loop?"

"The loop, Drover. Everyone knows what the loop is."

"You mean the loop in a cowboy's rope?"

"No, that's not what I mean at all. I'm talking about the Loop of Communication."

"You mean . . . ropes can talk?"

For a moment, I didn't know what to say. "Let's drope it, Dropper."

"My name's Drover."

"I'm very much aware of your name. It comes up every time there's a disaster on the ranch."

"Yeah, but you called me 'Dropper.' It kind of hurts my feelings." He hung his head and sniffled.

"All right, I'm sorry I called you Dropper."

"Are you really?"

"No. And to be perfectly honest, I think Dropper would be a better name for you than Drover."

"I think it sounds dumb."

"That's the point."

"You mean . . ."

"Never mind. Do you realize what's going on here?"

He glanced around. "Where?"

"Here. There. All around you, right in front of your nose."

He crossed his eyes and . . . I couldn't believe this . . . he looked at the end of his nose. "Well, a big fly just landed on my nose, and he's green. But I still don't see the loop."

I swallowed my urge to go into a screaming fit. "The pickups, Drover, the pickups and stock trailers and horses. Do you understand why they're here?"

"You called me Drover. Thanks. It really means a lot when you call me by my real name."

"I'm fixing to call you . . . just answer the question."

"Well, let me think." He rolled his eyes around and scrunched up his lips. "They're here because . . . they're not somewhere else?"

"Okay, that's a start. If the pickups and so forth weren't here, they'd be somewhere else."

"Yeah, and if they were somewhere else, they wouldn't be here."

"Exactly my point. But let's look deeper. Why are they *here* instead of somewhere else?" I stood there for thirty seconds, waiting for the little ninny to come up with the answer. "I'm sorry, we're out of time. You've flunked your test."

"Wait, I've got it. They're here because . . ."

"Yes, yes?"

"They're here because . . . because . . ."

"Hurry up, Drover!"

"They're here because . . . out of all the places in the whole world, this is where they all came. And there's a whole bunch of places where they didn't go."

The air hissed out of my lungs and I found myself staring at the dirt. "I try to help you. I try to bring you into my conversations, and you give me meathead answers like that. You flunk, pal, and you can spend the rest of the day in your room—with your nose in the corner."

He stared at me with tragic eyes. "No, anything but that. I hate standing in the corner."

"Drover, I gave you five chances to come up with the right answer and you still couldn't do it. When you flunk a test, you have to take the punishment."

"One more chance. I'll get it this time. Can you give me a little hint?"

I thought it over. "Okay, one more chance and that's it. Here's the hint: they came to help Slim and Loper with the spring branding."

I know, it was more than a "little hint," but I wanted to get this mess over with. And, to be honest, I'd begun to have second thoughts about sending him to his room. Maybe that was too harsh a punishment.

Drover went into a pose of deep concentration while I tapped my toe and gazed up at the clouds. Then his eyes popped open and a smile washed over his mouth. "I've got it this time."

"Great. What's the answer?"

He puffed himself up and said, "Loper's pickup

has a busted spring and they're going to help him put on a brand-new one."

A heavy silence rolled over us. I stared into the huge emptiness of his eyes. He was grinning, so happy with himself for coming up with the answer. I didn't have the heart to tell him that he was three times dumber than a box of rocks. I pushed him aside and marched away as fast as I could go. I couldn't stand any more.

Behind me, he called out, "Did I pass? Are you proud of me?"

"Yes. No. I don't care. Don't ever speak to me again."

Whew! I got away just in time. I've said this before but I'll say it again: that's a weird little mutt.

By this time the cowboys had unloaded their horses and tightened their cinches, and they were standing in a circle around Loper and Slim. Loper was giving out the orders for the roundup, telling which riders to go to which parts of the pasture. I stood outside the circle for a few moments, then wiggled my way between a pair of legs and emerged inside the ring of cowboys.

There, I sat down and, well, gave them a grin that said, "Sorry I'm late. What's the plan?"

When I appeared on the scene, Loper stopped

in the middle of his sentence. His eyes came at me like . . . I don't know, like a two-pronged fork, I guess you would say. They didn't seem real friendly.

"Hank, we won't be needing your help. Stay out of the way and don't make a sound until we get the cattle penned."

What? Stay out of the . . . hey, what was the deal? First they'd planned a roundup without consulting me, and now they didn't want my help? I was astamished, shocked, and deeply wounded. I looked around the circle of faces (why were they all grinning?) and went to a tail-setting we call "I Can't Believe You're Serious." In this setting, the top 90 percent of the tail assumes a lifeless position, while the last few inches tap out a slow, mournful rhythm on the ground.

Tap . . . tap . . . tap.

I studied their faces again, and suddenly realized that they weren't going to use me in the roundup. They weren't even looking at me. They had cut me out of their plans, thrown me aside like an old boot. This was crazy! I mean, what's the reason for keeping a highly trained cowdog on the place if you're not going to let him use his talents? Over the years, I had proved myself . . .

Okay, maybe I'd messed up a time or two.

Stood in the wrong gate. Barked at the wrong time. Stirred up a cow or two. Caused a couple of, uh, stampedes. But, hey, I'd learned from my little lapses in judgment, and those experiences had made me an older dog, a wiser dog. I was sure I could control my savage instincts and be a productive member of the Team.

No more careless barking. No more picking fights with stupid . . . no more getting into childish scuffles with the cows, and yes, I had learned valuable lessons about standing in the middle of gates. I had graduated from the School of Hard Knots and was ready . . .

They left, I mean, just walked away and left me sitting there! I hadn't even finished pleading my case. They swung up into their saddles and rode off across the dew-covered pasture, and not one of them even bothered to look back and see that they had left me there . . . a broken dog, a dog who was no longer wanted.

CHAPTER THREE

Drover Gives Me an Idea

Okay, that was IT. I was finished with this ranch and the ungrateful people who lived on it. I had given them the best years of my life and *this* was the thanks I got. I had no choice but to resign my position as Head of Ranch Security, quit in disgrace, leave the hateful place, and spend the rest of my days wandering in the wilderness, eating bugs and grub worms.

I whirled around and was about to march off to a lonely exile in the wilderness, when I ran into someone. A cat. Where had he come from? Only seconds before, he'd been nowhere in sight, but now . . .

Have you ever noticed that at the very moment when you crave silence and wish to be alone with your thoughts, a cat shows up? I've noticed. It happens all the time around here. His name is Pete, and though he's just a dumb little ranch cat, he has a genius for showing up at exactly the wrong times. If he were anything but a cat, you might begin to wonder if he's really so dumb, but he is a cat, so that leaves just one explanation: dumb luck.

The little creep was incredibly lucky, and his good luck is always bad luck for me, because I have no use for a cat. I have no use for a cat even on a good day, and on a bad day, such as the one we're discussing, I'd sooner have warts than be in the company of a cat.

But there he was—purring, rubbing on anything that didn't kick him away, and wearing that insolent smirk that drives me nuts.

I greeted him with a withering glare. "What are you doing here, you little sneak?"

"Good morning, Hankie."

"Oh yeah? What's so good about it?"

"Well, the sun's up and the dew is sparkling on the grass."

"Big deal. It was the same yesterday and the day before. So what?"

"I noticed that we have a cowboy crew on the ranch, Hankie. Do you suppose they're going to round up the pasture?"

"Yes, I suppose they are. What's your point?"

He glanced around in a circle. "Well, Hankie, to be truthful, I was a little surprised that you didn't . . . go with them."

His words caused my lips to twitch, exposing two rows of long white fangs. "I didn't go with them, kitty, because I didn't want to."

He heaved a sigh of relief. "Oh good. I was so afraid that . . . well, the thought occurred to me that maybe . . . you weren't invited."

He started rubbing on my front legs. I moved a step backward. "Don't touch me, you little reptile. Of course I was invited. They begged me to go, but I had other things to do."

"Oh really? Such as?"

"Such as . . . the list is so long, I don't have time to discuss it. Furthermore, it's classified information and I'm not at liberty to reveal it to a cat. Sorry."

He sat down, wrapped his tail around his body, and began licking his paw with long slow strokes of his tongue. "It hurts to be left out, doesn't it?"

"I wouldn't know about that, Pete. For your information, the Head of Ranch Security is wired into everything that happens on this . . ." I stuck my nose into his face. "What are you getting at? Is there some point to this conversation, or are you merely wasting my time?"

"We cats are very observant, Hankie. We notice little details."

"Hurry up."

"We notice little details such as . . . a cowdog who isn't invited to help with the cow work."

"I've already told you . . ."

"Then a long face and a look of deepest despair."

"Lies, Pete."

He looked at me with his weird yellow eyes. "They left you out, Hankie, and now you're feeling worthless and unwanted."

A growl began rumbling in depths of my throat, and in the back of my mind, I could hear the voice of Data Control: "Target is acquired and the weapon is ready for launch! Stand by for countdown." Every muscle in my enormous body was tense and ready for the launch. "Three! Two! One!"

I buried the little snot under the missile of my body, I mean, I rolled him up in a ball. But, you know, the funny thing about cats is that they never stay buried for long, so it came as no surprise, no great shock that he managed to . . . uh . . . wiggle out of the grisp of my grasp and buzzsaw my face with his claws. But that merely poured gasoline upon the embers of my righteous anger and made me even more determined to . . .

BZZZZZZZT!

A guy forgets how much damage a sniveling little cat can do with those claws, but the impointant point is that I bulled my way through his defensive measures, took my lumps, and kept truckin', sending the Kitty Army into blind, cowardly retreat. I chased him for twenty yards and ran him up a chinaberry tree.

It was beautiful, delicious. Poetry in motion. A magnificent symphony of Pure Dogness. I'm not sure the Security Division has ever known triumph on such a grand scale.

Standing at the base of the tree, I looked up and yelled, "And let that be a lesson to you!"

"Enjoy the roundup, Hankie."

"I will, and you enjoy the tree."

And with that stinging reply, I marched away from the tree, leaving Kitty Kitty sitting in the rubble of his own shubbles. Shambles. Sitting in the ramble of his own shambles. Sitting in the rubble of his own . . . phooey.

The point is that I had delivered the cat another humiliating defeat, and no dog could have been prouder. I held my head at a triumphant angle and . . . my nose was killing me! I sat down near the saddle shed and felt a cloud of gloom moving across my mind. Not only had I been cut out of the roundup work, but the cat had almost cut off my nose. Things had gone from bad to awful.

Just then, Drover walked up. "I heard a bunch of noise. What . . ." He stared at the wounds on my nose. "Gosh, what happened?"

I told him the whole miserable story. "The cowboys have lost confidence in me, Drover, and now I feel worthless and useless. I thought that thrashing the cat might brighten my day, but . . . well, you can see how that turned out."

"Yeah, he brightened your nose."

"Exactly. He brightened my nose with blood and made a gloomy day even gloomier." I stood up and began pacing. "And now my whole life seems pointless. I just wish there was something I could to do to show the cowboys . . ." I stopped pacing and stared at three mounds of fresh dirt in the middle of the corral gate. "Drover, come here and look at this."

He walked over to the dirt piles and sniffed them. "I'll be derned, gopher mounds. I guess there's a gopher digging underground. I hope the cows don't trip when they go through the gate."

I stared at him. "What did you just say?"

"I said, I hope the gophers don't trip . . . I hope the cows don't dig . . . oh drat, I can't remember."

"Drover, you may have just come up with a brilliant idea!"

"I did?"

"Yes, I know that sounds unlikely, that you'd come up with a brilliant idea, but listen to this." My mind was soaring by this time and I started pacing. "Where gophers dig, they leave the surface undisturbed, but the ground beneath the surface is a maze of tunnels and shafts, right?"

"I guess so."

"Okay, listen closely. What happens when a

herd of large animals walks across that surface?"

"I don't know. They step on a gopher?"

"No. Their hooves break through the surface and they fall into the gopher tunnel."

"Yeah, but . . ."

"Don't you get it? Nobody knows how deep those tunnels go. Why, they might go for miles and miles, right into some boiling pit at the center of the earth."

"Well, I don't think . . ."

"Just imagine, Drover, what would happen if all the cattle on this ranch plunged to their deaths in a bottomless gopher tunnel. Loper would be broke. Slim would be out of a job, and so would we."

"Yeah, but . . ."

I marched over to him and whapped him on the back. "Congratulations, son, you've just given me a way of redeeming myself!"

"You mean . . ."

"Yes. I'll stand in the gate and make sure that we don't lose any cattle in the Bottomless Gopher Tunnel."

"Yeah, but Loper told you . . ."

"He didn't notice the gopher evidence, Drover, and that's why we're here, to save Our People from their own errors and mistakes. Loper was careless, his mind was on other things." I stepped back and gave him a broad smile. "What do you think of that, soldier?"

"Well, it sounds . . . it sounds a little crazy."

"Crazy! Hey, this was your idea and I'm trying to . . ." Just then, I heard the sound of cattle in the distance. "Shhh. Listen. The cowboys are coming in with the herd. We haven't a moment to spare. Quick, to the corral gate!"

"See you later!"

CHAPTER FOUR

A Small Error
in Judgment

We moved our troops ten feet to the north, and there, in the middle of the open gate, we established the lines of battle. But when I glanced around, it occurred to me that some of our troops were missing. I took a head-count and . . . hmmm, we appeared to be one dog short. I counted again and . . . suddenly remembered that Drover's last words to me had been, "See you later."

Do you see the meaning of this? You'll be shocked. No, maybe you won't, because it was Typical Drover. See, the little never-sweat had seen some hard work looming on the horizon and had left the country. I directed my gaze toward the machine shed and, sure enough, there he stood in the crack between the two big sliding doors—watching me.

I yelled, "All right, pal! Go ahead and hide from responsibility. I'll see you later, after I receive my award for heroism."

He vanished inside the barn. That was okay. I would do better without him anyway. If he'd stayed around, I would have had to listen to him moan and groan, and answer his foolish questions about the assignment. He thought this was a "crazy idea"? My best response was not to argue, but merely to prove him wrong.

What did he know about gophers? Nothing. But I knew a lot. They're rodents who spend their whole lives underground. We very seldom see them because . . . well, because they spend their whole lives underground, and maybe it's obvious that you never see an animal that lives . . . never mind.

They dig these underground tunnels, and every three or four feet, they push their dirt outside the tunnel, creating the piles of soil we refer to as "gopher mounds."

What isn't so obvious about gophers is that they're destructive little brutes. Where they dig, the ground becomes softer than the soil nearby, creating a situation the cowboys refer to as "rotten ground." When a horse moves across "rotten ground," his feet can break through the surface, causing him to stumble or even fall.

And we've already discussed what might happen if a herd of cows walked over a piece of ground that had been burrowed and booby-trapped by a villainous little gopher. Don't forget, he'd done his mischief right in the middle of the *corral gate*.

It's pretty impressive that a dog would know so much about wildlife, isn't it? You bet. Ordinary mutts never take the time to memorize the names and habits of the various faunas and floras on their ranches. In fact, a lot of your ordinary mutts don't even have a ranch to supervise. All they have is a yard in town or a front porch, and what's to memorize about a front porch? June bugs? Buzzing flies? Maybe a mouse, if they're lucky?

That's why they spend most of their time sleeping and don't know beans about wildlife. Me, I take pride in knowing every little detail about every little creature that inhabits my country, right down to the ants.

You want to know about ants?

They're tiny bugs. They live in a hole in the ground and work a twelve-hour day. Darkness falls and those guys are gone, back in the hole. Their sleeping quarters are very crowded, with bugs stacked on top of bugs, and no doubt the place stinks of sweating ants.

They will eat almost anything: seeds, leaves,

crumbs, and grasshopper legs. They seem to be very fond of grasshopper legs, and almost any day in the spring or summer, you'll see an ant trying to drag one back to the den. These grasshopper "drumsticks" are much bigger than the ants who carry them, and some dogs wonder why an ant would go to the trouble to heave and tug a piece of food that's ten times bigger than the guy who's going to eat it.

Are you shocked that I know the answer? Heh heh. Here's the scoop on grasshopper drumsticks. Ants eat 'em on Thanksgiving Day instead of turkey legs, for the simple reason that a turkey leg would never fit inside an ant den.

Oh, one last detail about ants. They love pic-

nics. They're too stingy to hold their own, so they invade the picnics of others. Marching in long columns, just as though they'd been invited, they move into the picnic ground and set up shop. They are particularly fond of sandwiches, ice cream, and cake crumbs. In fact, they'll steal any kind food except pickled okra.

You never see an ant eating pickled okra.

So there you are, a pretty amazing lesson on ants—what they do, what they eat, and why you often see them dragging huge grasshopper drumstick-legs back to their holes. Actually, this is only a tiny part of my knowledge of ants, but we're out of time and need to get back to . . .

What were we discussing before we got involved in Ant Lore? I have a feeling that it was pretty important and that we need to get on with the story, but at this moment I can't . . . hmmmmm.

WAIT! Hold everything, stop, halt. We were right in the middle of a very important mission to keep the cows out of the corral and save the entire herd from plunging into a bottomless gopher hole. Are you ready? Okay, here we go, back to the corral gate.

Yes, this was a very important assignment, and it was a good thing that my interrogation of Drover had brought this crucial Gopher Information to our attention. It appeared that I had gotten it just in time to avoid a terrible disaster.

But I would have to hurry if I wanted to check things out before the cows came in. The bawling of the herd was growing louder and . . .

Huh? Cows? They had already arrived at the gate? Well, that was too bad. We had taken this gate out of service and they could just bug off and wait. (A little humor there. Bug off, ants. Get it? Ha ha.)

Why were they gathering around the gate and staring at me? How can a dog concentrate on his business when he's got fifteen dull-eyed cows gawking at him? He can't. It's terribly distracting.

I glared up at the circle of eyes. "Look, we're doing repairs and we're not ready for you yet. Anyone with half a brain could see that. Take a hike. Take a powder. You can't use this gate until I do a Gopher Search."

They didn't move, but continued staring at me.

"What part of 'Go away' don't you understand? Buzz off. Scram. Beat it. Nobody passes until I give the word." They didn't move. "Okay, you don't seem to take hints, so take this!"

Heh heh. Boy, did I give those cows a surprise. I threw myself at them, a lightning bolt of . . .

"Hank, get out of the gate!"

33

... a lightning bolt of flashing teeth, snapping jaws, flaming eyes, and ferocious barks that ...

"Hank, move!"

... sent them scattering in all directions like a covey of ...

"Idiot! Stop barking!"

... fluttering quail.

"Hold the herd, boys, they're gonna run!"

Yes sir, I got the point across. I hated to be rude, but how else can you communicate with a bunch of brainless cows? I mean, we weren't discussing

34

physics. It was a very simple message: "We're making repairs. You can't pass through the gate until . . . "

Gee whiz, those cattle were really spooked, running in all directions, almost like a . . . uh . . . stampede or something. Maybe I'd come on a little strong with my message, but when a guy's big and tough and about half-mean, sometimes he forgets . . . and, oops, it appeared that the cowboys were whipping and spurring to hold the herd . . . and yelling in angry tones . . . and crashing through the willows and tamaracks along the . . .

This was looking more and more like . . . well, a genuine stampede. Gee, what had gotten the cattle so . . .

HUH?

Suddenly, in a flash of blinding light, I realized that I was . . . oh brother . . . standing right in the middle of the gate, the very place I had been warned not to stand. And even worse, it appeared that my actions had caused . . .

Gulp.

How had this happened? I hadn't tried to cause problems. I'd been trying to help, for crying out loud! An ordinary mutt would have slept through the whole thing, but me, I had volunteered for extra duty, I'd walked the Extra Mile to help the cowboys and to save the cattle from . . .

Gulp.

Okay, we had big problems here. BIG PROB-
LEMS.

Damage Control. I began rehearsing my story.
"Slim, Loper . . . I know this looks pretty bad, and
I know what you're thinking. You gave me strict
orders to stay out of the gate and not to bark at
the cattle, and before we go any further, let me
state for the record that I agreed 100 percent with
those orders. Honest. No kidding.

"But what you didn't see and couldn't have
known was that . . . see, there were these gopher
mounds right in the middle of the gate, three of
them, to be exact, I just thought . . ."

Oh brother. I would never be able sell that story.
I was cooked. Fried. Toasted. They would kill me.
The only question was, would they use a firing
squad, a hangman's rope, or strangle me with their
bare hands?

Fellers, it was time for me to lay low and wait
for the storm to pass.

CHAPTER FIVE

Laying Low

W ho said I had to stick around for the scary part? I mean, what kind of dunce would hang around to be screeched at and possibly amputated from the face of the earth? Why couldn't I just vanish? Drover did it all the time, so why not me?

Yes, by George, there's a time to stand your ground and take your medicine, and there's a time to leave the medicine for the dogs who are too sick to run. Me? I could run, fellers, and that's just what I did. I whirled around, threw all engines into Turbo Five, sprayed sand with all four feet, and went streaking away on a course that would take me straight to the feed barn.

Remember the feed barn? It was a small structure made of cedar posts, old lumber, and roofing tin, located at the west end of the corrals. The cowboys used it for storing horse feed and bales of alfalfa hay. I often used it as a hiding place when . . . well, when Sally May got mad at me. It's hard to believe that a ranch wife would ever get mad at her very own Head of Ranch Security, but she did. And fairly often too.

The feed barn was a great place to hide because, if you'll recall, the door into the barn was warped at the bottom, just enough so that a desperate dog could wiggle and squeeze himself inside.

And that's just what I did, swiggled and wheezed myself through the crack, and took refuge behind a stack of hay bales. There, I spent an incredibly boring four hours, snapping at flies and listening to every sound and noise from the world outside.

Here's a recap of what I heard. It took the cowboys about forty-five minutes to make another sweep of the pasture, and they finally succeeded in penning the cattle in the corral. It saddens me to report that the cattle entered the corrals through the Gopher-Trapped Gate. I peeked out the door to confirm this, because . . . well, I fully expected to see the first ten cows plunge into a bottomless tunnel.

They didn't even stumble, which really burned me up, and it even suggested that maybe I had, uh, overestimated the danger of . . . they got lucky. What else can you say? On another day, that same bunch of cattle might have . . .

Let's talk about something else. There isn't a dog alive who enjoys admitting that he was wrong, and I enjoy it even less than most. In fact, I hate it.

The point is that, after all their yelling and screeching about me standing in the gate, the cowboys penned the herd and started branding. With two cowboys using their ropes to heel and drag the calves to the branding fire, they finished the work in about three hours.

Sometime around eleven-thirty, I heard the neighbors saying good-bye and loading their horses into the trailers. As the hum of the pickups faded into the distance, I crept out from behind the haystack and slithered myself through the crack in the door. Slim and Loper would be in a better humor now that the work was done, so this seemed a good time for me to . . . well, patch up old relationships, relationships that had been bruised and damaged by recent events.

For sure I would have to look sad and sorry, very sorry, for whatever small part I had played in the, uh, tragedy.

They had unsaddled their horses and were standing just outside the saddle shed. As I walked toward them, looking very sad and sorry, I over-heard their conversation.

Slim: "If you'd tied him up, it never would have happened."

Loper: "Hindsight's twenty-twenty, and yours may even be better than that."

Slim: "Well, I could have told you. Give a ding-bat a chance to prove that he's a dingbat, and he'll do it every time."

Loper: "If you're so smart, why didn't you say something about it?"

Slim hitched up his jeans. "Loper, you take sug-gestions about as well as a rock. Besides, you're the boss around here. I ain't paid for thinking."

"Huh. Good thing too." Loper scowled up at the sky. "I hate to tie up a dog and it shouldn't be nec-essary. If we're going to keep dogs on the ranch, they ought to be taught to obey a command."

Slim's mouth dropped open. "Obey a command. Now, that's a real new idea. Who's going to be the teacher?"

"I had you in mind."

"That's what I figured, but since I have to do all the work on this place, that don't leave much time for schooling dogs. And you sure wouldn't qualify."

"What makes you think so?"

Slim slouched against the door. "Loper, I'd like to meet the dog you trained. After you got through with him, he'd need to spend six weeks with a psychiatrist, and you know why? 'Cause you ain't got enough patience to boil an egg, much less train a dog."

Loper glared at him. "So what do you suggest?"

"Well, the easiest thing would be to sell the ranch and throw in the dog as a bonus."

Loper barked a laugh. "Well, I hadn't thought of that. What else?"

Slim brought out his pocketknife and started cleaning his fingernails. "I was listening to the radio yesterday and heard an ad. Some feller's coming to town to hold an Obedience School for dogs. It starts tomorrow morning, but you have to register your dog this afternoon at the court-house."

"Keep talking."

"Well, my first thought was that we might try to enroll *you*, but I don't think they'd drop their standards that low." Slim chuckled at his joke.

Loper heaved a sigh. "Slim, hurry up."

"Well, here's a guy who knows something about training dogs and he's coming to Twitchell. You could load up Birdbrain and take him to school. It only costs twenty-five bucks."

Loper thought it over. "Okay, it's worth a try. Only I'll be busy."

Slim's eyes came up. "Busy doing what?"

"I'll be busy being busy. This was your big idea, buddy, you take the dog. Oh, and don't go dropping him off and slipping away to the pool hall. You stay and watch. Maybe it's not too late for you to learn something too." Loper's face lit up with a grin. "Like I've said before, being the boss has a few advantages."

"Loper, I've got fifteen thousand things to do!"

"Get him enrolled this afternoon—take him with you so he doesn't try to hide. And don't forget to wash out the vaccine guns."

Loper gave him a wink and walked away, leaving Slim alone with a stunned expression on his face. Slim closed up his knife and started muttering to himself.

"Well, that'll teach me to come up with an idea. By grabs, next time I'll just keep my trap shut." He cupped his hand around his mouth and yelled, "It sure don't pay to use your brain on this outfit!"

Loper walked on to the house.

That was a pretty interesting conversation, don't you think? I thought it was very interesting, because it revealed that the cowboys had gotten fed up with Drover's careless behavior and were going to *send him off to school*. Did you notice that they'd called him "dingbat" and "Birdbrain"? I had called him those names many times myself, and we're talking about dozens or hundreds of times, and yes, it was high time that somebody tried to teach him something.

Hey, this was great news, the best news of the week. If there was any dog in Texas who needed to go to a school for dingbats and birdbrains, it was Drover. I put all thoughts of sadness and remorse behind me, held my head at a proud angle, and marched up to Slim. I wanted him to know that I supported his decision 100 percent.

When he saw me, his eyebrows lifted. "Well, speak of the devil and here he comes."

What was that supposed to mean? Well, it didn't matter because I already understood the overall plan for the afternoon. Drover would get trapped and captured and hauled off to town, and guess who would lead Slim to Drover's secret hiding place.

Heh heh. Me. Because I knew exactly where to find the little weenie. Heh heh. He should have known better than to sneak off in the middle of an important job.

Slim scratched me behind the ears. "Pooch, stick with me. We've got things to do."

44

You bet I'd stick with him. Routing Drover out of the machine shed would be a real pleasure.

I followed Slim to the stock tank and waited for him to wash out the vaccine guns. This was terrific. I could almost hear Drover's reaction. He would moan and cry, plead and beg, and then I would have the pleasure of saying, "Drover, I've warned you and warned you about this disobedience thing, but you didn't listen. It's gone far enough and now they're finally taking some action."

Have we ever discussed the Four Most Delicious Words in the world? Maybe not, so here they are: "I told you so."

Slim washed out the vaccine guns and put them away in the saddle shed. He gave the horses some grain and hay, and together we walked to his pickup, which was parked in the shade near the gas tanks. At first, I was a little surprised that he wanted to drive around to the machine shed, but then it made sense. He didn't want to carry the hysterical Drover a hundred yards to the pickup, so yes, parking the pickup right beside the machine shed doors was a shrewd decision.

He opened the pickup door and told me to load up. No problem there. With a mighty leap, I sprang up on the seat and took the Shotgun Position beside the open window. Slim got in and we drove around the front of the house. Loper was standing out on the porch.

Slim yelled out, "I ain't done with this. I plan to file a protest!"

Loper grinned and waved good-bye.

We drove past the house and up a little hill to the place where the road forks, with the left fork leading to the machine shed. Slim stopped the pickup and studied me with narrowed eyes. "I think I'll roll up that window, Hankie. I'd hate for you to fall out."

Well . . . sure, fine. I mean, it was a short drive to the machine shed, but if he was worried about my safety . . . you know, sometimes a guy gets to thinking that the cowboys don't care about their dogs, but then they do some little thing that lets you know that they really do. I found it very sweet and touching that Slim was so worried about me falling out the window that he took the time to roll it up. I mean, there for a second, it almost brought tears to my eyes.

He leaned across the seat and rolled up the window, and I was so overcome with emotion that I licked him on the ear.

"Quit it!"

Okay, maybe I shouldn't have licked his ear, but sometimes a guy just has to express his feelings.

Slim put the pickup in first gear and let out on the clutch. I waited for him to steer the pickup to the left, toward the machine shed, but ... hmmm. He kept driving north, toward the mailbox. Okay, before we got involved with capturing Mister Half-Stepper, Slim wanted to check the mail, right?

That made sense. Another good decision.

We drove to the mailbox and ... huh? Turned left? And started driving west on the county road?

Hey, what was going on around here? I barked and tried to communicate a very important message: "Drover's in the machine shed. I know, I saw him myself. I can lead you right to him. This road doesn't lead to the machine shed. It goes ..."

HUH?

This was the road ... to town!

CHAPTER SIX

The Dead Squirrel Mystery

Oh treachery! Oh twisted lies and false promises and half-truths!

Do you see what he was doing? After recruiting me to rat on Drover, after using all kinds of trickery and underhanded methods, he . . . this was an outrage!

Are you shocked? I was shocked. The magnitude of this swindle left me breathless. Slim and Loper had planned it this way all along, only they had used secret code words (Birdbrain and dingbat, remember?) to fool me into thinking that Drover would be the victim.

Well, if he thought I was just going to sit there while he kidnapped me and hauled me off to town, he didn't understand the resourceful mind of a dog.

I turned to the window and prepared to launch myself . . .

Huh?

Okay, remember when Slim stopped the pickup and rolled up the window? Oh foolish me, I had supposed that he did it out of concern for my safety. What a cruel joke. It was clear now that he had rolled it up as part of a well-planned, wicked plot to steal me away from my ranch and home.

And you know what? He had pulled it off. I had been completely taken in. He had used my trusting nature against me and there wasn't a thing I could do about it but sit back and enjoy the ride, only I was determined NOT to enjoy the ride.

I turned a pair of laser-beam eyes on Slim, and with glares and facial expressions, I said, "You tricked me and I can hardly express the depths of my sense of outrage."

He didn't even look at me. You know what he was doing? He was humming a tune and steering the pickup in a wild pattern from one side of the road to the other. Was he trying to get us killed or something?

He must have felt my eyes on him, because he turned and gave me a grin. "I'm smashing grasshoppers, pooch. They're thick as fleas this year, and a guy might as well do some pest control while he's driving."

Oh, that was brilliant, smashing grasshoppers with his pickup tires.

You see what I have to put up with on this ranch? We have grown men on the payroll who have nothing better to do than drive like maniacs so they can bump off a few grasshoppers on the county road!

Oh brother.

Slim and I had nothing more to say to each other, and a frigid silence moved into the space between us. The trip to town was not a pleasant experience.

He pulled up to a big brick building on Main Street in Twitchell and shut off the motor. "Well, this is the courthouse. Hankie, you might as well brighten up and try to enjoy this. Who knows, it might turn out to be fun."

Okay, I would try to brighten up, not because I was a slave to "fun" but because . . . well, brooding about it wouldn't do one bit of good. It was perfectly clear that Slim didn't care about my wounded feelings, so I might as well try to make the best of it. Maybe it wouldn't be so bad, this school for dumb dogs.

He unbuckled his belt and slipped it off his

jeans, made a loop out of it and dropped the loop around my neck. "Just to be safe, we're going to use a little restraining device. I'd hate for you to get lost in the big city."

Very funny.

We walked past a row of tall Chinese elm trees in front of the courthouse. Straining at my leash, I tugged Slim toward the first tree and gave it a good sniffing. Hmmm. Very interesting. The trunk of that tree contained the following message: "This is my tree. MINE, you understand? So shove off, jerk. If I ever catch you around my tree, I'll wreck your nose. Signed, Muggsie."

Oh yeah? Well, I had a little message for Muggsie, but Slim pulled the leash and we continued our walk toward the courthouse. As we drew closer, I began to appreciate the size of this building. It was huge! I mean, we're talking about three stories high, much bigger than the machine shed or any other building I'd seen in the country. What did they do in that place?

Even Slim seemed impressed. He craned his skinny neck and looked up at the top row of windows. "It would hold a pretty big bunch of hay, wouldn't it?" But he didn't gawk at the building for long. See, without his belt, his jeans started slipping down on his hips and he had to jerk them up.

51

Tee hee. Served him right.

We walked up the steps and went through a pair of heavy doors. The instant we entered that place, I started having bad feelings about it. The air was cool and had an odd smell. I can't describe it, only to say that it was unnatural. There wasn't a trace of animals, dirt, trees, wood, wildflowers, none of the smells you'd find on a ranch.

And those long stony hallways . . . it was so quiet in there, you could hear every sound, every footstep echoing all around you. Fellers, this place was just a little bit spooky.

Slim paused in front of a plaque on the wall and read several rows of lettering. "There we go. Basement. Come on, pooch."

He led me to a stairway that went down about six feet and then turned back to the right. I couldn't see where the stairs were leading, only that they were going down into some kind of . . . well, dark pit. Sort of like a dungeon. This contributed to my bad feeling and I decided not to go.

GULK.

Okay, I would go, but not happily and not willingly. He dragged me down the stairs, is the point, and just as I had feared, this so-called basement was no place a dog would ever choose to spend any time: cold, gloomy, and as silent as a tomb. Slim studied the signs over several doors and headed toward one that said "Coffee Room."

Well, that was sounding a little better. I mean, where you find coffee you find people and conversation and something besides shadows and echoes. We walked through the door and saw a man sitting at a table. His head was down and he seemed to be writing on a pad of paper.

Right away, I noticed something peculiar about his hair. It looked more like fur than hair.

Slim said, "Knock knock?"

The man's head came up and . . . yipes! He was wearing these thick glasses, see, and behind the glasses were these two big green eyes, and we're not talking about normal eyes, fellers, but huge eyes. Frog eyes or fish eyes. Monster eyes.

That was all I needed to know. If that guy had anything to do with Obedience School, I was checking out!

GULK.

Or maybe not. Don't forget, Slim had me on a leash.

The man smiled and introduced himself as Rudy Something. Uh oh, he had a gold tooth. Never trust a man with a gold tooth, I always say, and this was not looking good. But then he took off his glasses and . . . well, his eyes looked better now, more normal and less like . . . ha ha . . . sometimes a pair of glasses will . . . I don't know what they do, but they make the eyes look kind of ghoulish. Anyway, I felt some better when he took them off.

"Well!" said Rudy. "I see you've brought a little friend to enroll in our school."

"Yes sir, and I hope you can teach him something. The rest of us haven't had much luck."

"It's all technique. Technique and patience. You'll be amazed."

Rudy wrote down some information on his pad and had Slim fill out a form. Then he took Slim's check and gave him a little booklet that he was supposed to read before school started in the morning. Slim looked at the cover and said, *"The Well-Adjusted Dog?"*

Rudy smiled. "That's right, and it's even autographed." He made some notes on his pad of paper, and once again I found myself studying his hair. I hopped my front paws up on the table and leaned toward it to get a better view.

"Hank!"

Rudy chuckled. "He's all right. We're going to be friends, I can already tell. Now, let's see. His name is Hank?" Rudy wrote that down. "And he is a . . . what's the breed?"

"Soup hound."

"Mixed breed, we call it." He wrote that down. "And does Hank have any physical handicaps or abnormalities?"

"No, just a few mental problems."

Rudy got a chuckle out of that. "So Hank's a ranch dog? We don't get many of those."

While Rudy was bent over the desk, I managed to run a Sniffonalysis on his hair. Just as I had suspected, there was something peculiar about it. It not only looked odd, but I detected something unusual in the scent. It just didn't smell right. Did I dare press this investigation a little further?

I rolled my eyes toward Slim and saw that he wasn't watching. He was hitching up his jeans again, so I leaned closer, made pinchers of my front teeth, and sort of . . .

You won't believe this. You absolutely won't believe it, but I'll tell it anyway. Rudy drew back his head and I found myself holding . . .

No wonder I'd been suspicious of his hair. *The guy had been wearing a squirrel on his head!* It came off and now the dome of his head was as smooth as an egg.

For a long moment of heartbeats, we stared into each other's eyes. Rudy's pleasant smile turned into a crooked snarl. "Give me that!" He leaped up from the chair and made a grab for my prize.

Maybe I should have given it back, but . . . I don't know, when he lunged at me like that, I just had this instinct to hang on to it.

I mean, how often does a dog catch a squirrel in the basement of a courthouse . . . on a man's head? This was one for the record books and I wasn't anxious to give it up.

Slim almost had a stroke. His face turned bright red and he yanked it out of my jaws. Bad idea. Something ripped. He handed the thing back to Rudy. "Mister, I'm sure sorry about this."

Rudy snatched it away, looked it over, and pitched it onto the table. "Maybe you're right about the dog. We'd be glad to refund your money."

"Nope, the boss said to bring him."

"I see." A smile of ice formed on Rudy's mouth. "In that case, we'll see you tomorrow morning at nine o'clock."

I thought that was the end of it, but it wasn't, and this last part is really strange. The guy fixed his eyes on me, leaned toward me with his bald head shining in the light, and . . . barked. I'm not kidding, he actually BARKED at me.

We left the room in a hurry.

CHAPTER SEVEN

I Begin Plotting
My Escape

Outside, we paused long enough for Slim to hitch up his jeans and wipe the beads of sweat off his face. He took a big gulp of air and looked down at me. "Bonehead. That was his hairpiece, and I'm just lucky he didn't make me buy him a new one."

Hairpiece? You mean . . . like a wig or something? Oh. Gee. Well, it had sure looked like a squirrel to me. Smelled like a squirrel too.

We walked down the steps in front of the courthouse and started toward the pickup. Slim said, "You know, I don't know as I've ever seen a grown man bark at a dog before. It makes you wonder, don't it?"

Right. And they wanted to send me to that guy's school?

By the time we reached the pickup, Slim had loosened up a bit and had a twinkle in his eye. "Hank, that stunt ain't likely to get you into Phi Beta Clapper, but I've got to admit it was pretty funny. Heh. I can't wait to tell Loper."

Good. I hoped they got twenty-five dollars' worth of laughs out of it, because . . . well, you'll find out.

We pulled into ranch headquarters and parked below the house, in the shade of the elm trees. Slim climbed out, hitched up his pants, and put on his belt. He was still chuckling to himself and seemed to be in a cheerful mood.

Good. It was all part of my plan, and to add sauce to the gander, I put on a blank face that showed no wicked thoughts whatever, a false front that showed Happy Dog and Duh. (We use the Happy Dog and Duh Programs when we don't want them to know what's really going on inside our minds, don't you see.)

"Well, pooch, I've got a couple hours' work to do around here, then we'll go down to my place for the night. How does that sound?"

Oh great, swell, you bet. Duh. Just what I'd always wanted to do.

Did he think I didn't know his plan? He wanted me to spend the night at his shack so that he wouldn't have to search for me in the morning. Little did he know.

Slim hiked down to the corrals to work with a colt. I watched until he dropped out of sight, then I went ripping up the hill to the machine shed. On the gravel drive in front of the shed, I executed a smooth landing and dived through the crack between the big sliding doors.

It was pretty dark in there, but that didn't prevent me from . . . well, stumbling over paint cans, bolt boxes, cutting torch hoses, welding hoods, wads of baling wire, and fifty-seven thousand other articles of junk that Slim and Loper had left lying around on the shop floor. If you ask me, those guys are slobs and I almost broke my neck trying to pick my way through their junkyard. How's a dog supposed to make a Stealthy Entry into a barn full of . . .

The point is that my Stealthy Entry into the machine shed wasn't so stealthy. It was very noisy, in fact, but I can't be blamed for that.

After staggering and stumbling through acres of junk, I picked my way through the gloomy darkness and headed for the very backest corner. It had been years since I had ventured so deep into the shed, back into the area where Sally May stored old pieces of furniture and where Loper kept his

canvas-covered canoe and camping gear—relics from an almost-forgotten time in Loper's life, before children and bankers.

It was an eerie place, a kind of twilight zone where time stopped and the sun never shone. Very few dogs in the whole world had ever been there, or would have wanted to be there. I knew of only one: Drover. For you see, this was his Secret Sanctuary, the place where he came to flee from Reality.

"Drover? Hello?" I stopped and listened. Not a sound. "Drover, I know you're in here." I cocked my ear and waited. Nothing. I took another step, then another, until my eyes could barely make out the shape of a big stuffed chair, covered with a sheet. I squinted into the darkness, and slowly another shape began to take shape: a dog lying absolutely motionless on the seat of the chair.

This was either Drover or a statue of Drover. I was pretty sure that nobody in his right mind would bother to make a statue of such a weird little mutt, but . . . well, it didn't move and it sure looked like a statue. I moved closer and gave it a sniffing. Seconds later, the report came back from Data Control and flashed across the screen of my mind: "Live Dog."

"I see you, Drover. The game's finished. You can come out now."

"Oh drat."

"Did you actually think you could hide from me?"

"Well, it was worth a try."

"Heh. Your Statue Trick might have worked on some dogs, son, but it was your misfortune to be tracked down by the Head of Ranch Security."

"Darn. What are you doing in here?"

"Oh, I just wanted to, uh, look around and, you know, see this place where you . . ." I glanced over both shoulders and lowered my voice. "Drover, may I confide in you? I mean, can we speak dog-to-dog?"

"Oh yeah, 'cause I'm a dog and so are you."

"I know, but I'm talking about something more profoon than our mere dogness."

"I don't wear perfume."

"I'm aware that you don't wear perfume. If you did, you wouldn't smell so bad."

"Yeah, and I'd be sneezing my head off. Perfume really stirs up my allergics." He sneezed. "See whad I beed? Just the bention of berfube bakes be sdeeze."

I closed my eyes and counted to ten. "Drover, let's begin again. May I confide in you? May I tell you a tale of woe?"

"Oh sure, 'cause I've got one too. They chopped it off when I was a pup."

"Are you trying to be funny?"

"I don't think so. There's nothing funny about a stub tail."

"Please dry up and listen to my tale of woe. We can begin with a simple statement of fact. Drover, I have a problem."

"Yeah, I figured."

"That's why I'm here."

"That's what I thought."

I gave him a steely glare. "Do you want to hear my story or not?"

"I already know. I heard 'em talking. They're going to send you to Obedience School, and I guess you don't want to go."

"Of course I don't want to go. Do you have any idea what happens at these so-called Obedience Schools?"

"Well, let me think. You have to be nice all the time? That wouldn't be so bad."

"Wouldn't be so bad! Okay, pal, you want to know about Obedience School?"

He was silent for a moment. "Well, I'm not sure. It isn't scary, is it?"

"You can decide that for yourself."

"I hate scary stories."

"Just listen. Here's the scoop on Doggie School." In the gloom of Drover's Secret Sanctuary, I began pacing back and forth. "First off, we can drop the business about it being a school. That's a joke. People don't send naughty dogs to a school, they send them to a DUNGEON. See, right in the center of downtown Twitchell, there's this old castle, built many years ago by a wicked king. It's a huge brooding mountain of stone with towers and drawbridges and all that other stuff you find with castles. And it's full of hooting owls and black cats and creatures that make terrible sounds in the night.

"That's where they're going to hold this so-called school. Angry dog owners drive up to the drawbridge with their naughty dogs, see, and this guy comes out of the castle to meet them. Description: eight feet tall, bulging muscles, menacing green eyes, crooked nose, and scars all over his face. When he laughs, birds fly away and snakes dive into holes, is how wicked his laugh is. Oh, and he carries a long whip . . . and he wears a dead squirrel on his head!"

I heard Drover gasp. "A dead squirrel!"

"Yes sir, because he has no hair, because it all fell out years ago. His heart is so wicked, it poisoned all his hair roots."

"Oh my gosh!"

I plunged on. "He collects all the naughty dogs and leads them into the castle, through long echoing hallways, and down a long flight of stairs. The deeper they go, the colder and darker it gets, until they reach . . . THE DUNGEON OF DOOM."

"The dungeon of doom! You mean . . ."

"Yes, Drover, the dungeon of doom. It's cold, damp, clammy. Water drips from the ceiling. The only light in the place comes from torches along the walls, and they cast eerie shadows, like dancing goblins. As you might imagine, all the poor little dogs are scared silly. They're glancing around with big moon-eyes and they start whining: 'Wait, we'll be good! We promise. Just let us go home and we'll never be naughty again!'"

I could see Drover's big moon-shaped eyes, so I kept going. "But the Dungeon Keeper just laughs and pops his whip. It's the most chilling laugh you ever heard, Drover, and as it echoes through the depths of the . . . "

Drover covered his eyes with his paws. "Stop, I can't stand any more!"

"Very well, we'll leave it at that, but now maybe you can understand why I'm here. Drover, I'm not going to that school and I've come to ask permission to use your Secret Sanctuary."

"No thanks."

"I'm sure you won't have a problem with that."

"No thanks."

"I mean, it's kind of an honor when the Head of . . . did you just say 'no thanks'?"

"About five times."

I marched over to him and gave him a menacing glare. "When you said 'no thanks,' did you mean you won't share your hiding place with the best friend you've ever had?"

He uncovered his eyes. "Well, I kind of like being alone. It's quieter that way."

"What are you saying, Drover? Are you saying that I'm a noisy dog?"

"Well, people are always yelling at you. It hurts my ears."

The air hissed out of my lungs and I stared at him in disbelief. "You won't give me permission to hide in here?"

"Well . . . I hate to put it that way."

"But that's what you meant?"

"Sort of."

I paced away from him and . . . what was that thing lurking in the darkness, a tricycle? What a dumb place to park a tricycle! I picked myself up and spoke to him in my darkest, sternest tern of vone.

"Very well, Drover, you leave me no choice. As of this moment, I am stripping you of all rank and taking over your Secret Sanctuary!"

CHAPTER EIGHT

Drover's Secret Sanctuary

A moment of deathly silence fell over the place, then Drover started bawling. "I don't want any company! I want to be alone so I can hide from the world!"

"I'm sorry, son, but you happen to have the best hiding place on the ranch, and I happen to need it. Now, we're going to make some changes around here. First off, get out of Sally May's chair."

He stopped blubbering and stared at me. "You mean . . ."

"I mean you ought to be ashamed of yourself, plopping down on her chair."

"Well, she left it in here . . ."

"Drover, she didn't leave it in here so you could

68

paw it and leave ugly dog hairs all over it. Now get down, immediately."

He whined and moaned, and hopped down. "Where will I sit?"

"I don't know. There's a tricycle over there. Try it out."

"It's got a metal seat."

"I don't care." I hopped up into the chair and fitted my bohunkus into the soft folds of the cushion. "I see what you mean. This is a great chair."

"No fair, you stole my seat!"

"I didn't steal it. I'm merely putting it into service for The Cause. If you'll try to improve your attitude, maybe I'll share it with you."

"Not me. I'm getting out of here before the trouble starts. Bye."

And with that, the runt made his way to the big double doors and vanished into the light of day.

Well, with Drover gone, I had the place all to myself and that was no bad deal. When a guy is desperate for company and is down to the bottom of his list of friends, Drover can provide a certain degree of companionship, if you don't mind listening to him complain about his "bad leg," his allergies, his stub tail, and all the other things he moans about.

"Anyway, where were we? I don't remember,

but . . . hmm. Listen to those three words again, and say them fast: "Where were we, where were we?" Taken together, they make an odd combination of sounds, don't they? We not only have a repetition of W-words, but spoken rapidly, the words also take on the flavor of . . . well, nonsense. "Ware wurr wee, ware wurr wee." Do you suppose there's any way in the world we could work up a wacky little song out of those three words? What the heck, let's give it a shot.

Where Were We?

Where were we, where were we,
    and were we wearing tennies?
Where were we, where were we,
    and were we spending pennies?
Walking wacky warbler birds,
Wasting wanton weary words,
Warmly washing wardrobe things,
Wearing weasel waterwings.

Where were we, where were we,
    what was the weather doing?
Where were we, where were we,
    what weirdness was ensuing?
Watching weary walnut shells,

Witching weedy waterwells,
Waltzing walruses around,
Warming wafers on the ground.

Ware wurr wee, ware wurr wee,
    ware wurr wee ware ware ware.
Ware wurr wee, ware wurr wee,
    ware wurr wee ware ware ware.
Ware wee wurr, ware wee wurr,
Ware wee wurr wurr wee ware,
Ware wee wurr, ware wee wurr,
Ware wee wurr wurr ware.

Where were we, where were we,
    the waterwell was turning.
Where were we, where were we,
    the waffle wads were burning.
Warning wasps of weevil plots,
Weatherwise, it's not so hot,
Weakly wiring warden's house,
Whalebone corset for a mouse.

Where were we, where were we?
    I think we're weirdly finished.

What do you think? I know, it's kind of a strange
little song, but don't forget that our objective was

to see if it could be done, and by George, we did it. So there you are. Nobody ever said that a song had to make sense.

Now, where were we? (Don't sing, I'm just asking the question). Oh yes, alone in Drover's Secret Sanctuary, where I planned to hide out for several days. I was enjoying the silence and the pleasure of my own company. Maybe that sounds snobbish, but it happens to be the truth. I had the vast sweep of my own mind to keep me entertained, and who could ask for more than that?

The first thirty minutes flew by. I amused myself thinking great thoughts, and singing clever little songs, but then I found myself . . . well, cooped up in a musty machine shed and growing a little tired of my own company, to be perfectly honest. Or, to put it another way, I was dying of boredom.

At last, in desperation, I hopped down from the chair and went creeping through the . . . crash, bang . . . paint cans, cardboard boxes, and other articles of junk , and made my way to the strip of daylight that was showing between the big sliding doors. I poked my head outside and glanced around, and who should come hopping along but Drover himself. He appeared to be chasing a butterfly.

"Psssst! Hey Drover."

He stopped and glanced around in a circle. "Did someone call my name?"

"Over here. I have some great news: it's me!"

His eyes followed the sound of my voice. When he saw me, I'm sorry to report that his smile faded like a flower that had been sprayed with poison. Plop. "Oh. Hi."

"Drover, it's great to see you again. Hey, listen pal, I've got a terrific idea. Why don't you come back into the machine shed and we'll, uh, play some games and have a great time, huh? What do you think of that?"

He wagged his head from side to side. "We tried that and it didn't work. You stole my secret hiding place."

"Drover, I didn't exactly steal it and . . . look, I've got a new deal to propose. What's happened is history, water under the boat. The new deal is that we share your hideout, fifty-fifty, equal partners in the Business of Life. What do you say to that?"

"You stole my chair too."

"Chair? I don't remember . . . okay, the chair. Hey, we can work that out too, no problem. Check this out. Under the new deal, you get the chair."

He twisted his head to the side. I took this as a good sign. It meant that he was thinking over my deal. He said, "Yeah, but where would you sit—on the tricycle?"

"Are you crazy? That thing has a metal seat."

"Yeah, but when I said that, you said you didn't care."

Oops. I squeezed up a pleasant smile. "Good point, you nailed me on that. Ha ha. Okay, in a careless moment, while I was under a terrible emotional strain, I did in fact say that I didn't care. But Drover, it's different now. Under our new deal, I promise to care."

"About what?"

"About everything. Anything. Look, Drover, I don't want to say bad things about your hiding place, but . . . *what do you do in there,* hour after hour?"

He grinned. "Well, sometimes I count goats."

"Count goats? We don't have goats on this ranch."

"Yeah, I just make 'em up."

"Oh. Of course. But why count goats?"

He rolled his eyes up to the sky. "Well, if you count sheep, you'll fall sleep. If you count goats, you can stay awake."

I stared at him for a moment. "Oh yes. I hadn't thought of that. And I guess you, uh, want to stay awake, huh?"

"Yeah, I'm afraid to fall asleep in a dark place, 'cause I might disappear and never come back. I'd miss the ranch if I never came back."

"Well, sure, you bet. And Drover, we'd miss you too." There was another moment of awkward silence. "Don't you get bored, counting goats?"

"Well, you don't count by ones. You count the legs and divide by eight."

"Goats have four legs. Why would you divide by eight?"

"Oh, I don't know. I've always liked eight. It goes around in circles like an electric train and trains are fun."

I blinked my eyes and tried to think of something to say. "Well! This is very interesting, Drover, but to be perfectly honest, if I have to spend several days hiding in the machine shed, I'd rather not count goats."

"Elephants are fun too, but you have the count the trunk."

"I don't want to count anything. Look, I'm desperate. There's a real danger that I might die of boredom in there, so . . . well, I'm inviting you to share my company. Out of all the dogs in the world, Drover, I've chosen you."

"Gosh, that's nice."

"Thanks. Why are you backing away?"

"'Cause I can hear Slim coming and I don't want to get in trouble. Bye."

"Drover, come back here!" In a flash of white, he was gone. I was too stunned to move, but I had to move anyway. Slim was coming to capture me and haul me down to his shack, and I had to hide.

Never mind boredom. I was not going to that school!

CHAPTER NINE

Under Arrest!

You heard that conversation between me and Drover, right? Did any of it make sense to you? That was the weirdest conversation I'd ever heard! Counting goats? Counting their legs and dividing by eight?

Sometimes I worry about Drover. I mean, he's not only running loose in the world, but he's running loose on *my ranch*. I have to live with the mutt. We share an office and bedroom. Some people think we're friends. Oh well.

I didn't have time to think about Drover. I dived back into the machine shed and crept . . . clang bang . . . stumbled through the maze of junk and finally reached the Secret Sanctuary near the northwest corner. There in the gloomy darkness,

I hopped up on the seat of the chair and assumed the pose of the mysterious Sphincter, that huge statue carved out of desert rock by the ancient Egyppers.

With my head frozen above two extended front paws, I sat motionless and listened to sounds of approaching footsteps. One set of footsteps. Slim's.

I heard his voice outside. "Here, Hank! Come on, boy. Come to Uncle Slim." He waited a moment and called again, this time quite a bit gruffer. "Hank, come here! Hank? He smells a rat. Okay, Plan B."

He opened the big sliding doors and sunlight poured inside. Lucky for me, very little of the light reached my spot in the Secret Sanctuary. I had bad news for Slim. I wasn't fixing to show myself, and he could forget about me going to a school for dumb dogs.

He was about to learn how dumb I was. Heh heh.

He searched around the shed until he found a Co-op Dog Food sack that still had a few kernels of tasteless dry dog food in it. He smiled to himself. "This'll work." He carried the sack outside and started shaking it. "Supper time, come and get it! Come on, Hankie Boy, it's steak and taters!"

What a joke. I mean, it embarrassed me to sit there and watch a grown man make such a fool of himself. In the first place, even if I hadn't been wise to his schemes, I never would have fallen for that "steak and taters" hogwash. Didn't I know what came in a paper sack that had "CO-OP DOG FOOD" written on the side in big red letters? Hey, I'd spent my whole life eating that stuff, and I knew for a fact that it tasted only slightly better than firewood. Or soap.

"Steak and taters." That was pathetic.

This was going to be a long, discouraging evening for Slim. He would look all over ranch headquarters and yell himself hoarse trying to find me, but he would never think of looking in Drover's Secret Sanctuary . . . tee hee . . . because I'd never used it before. It was the last place on the ranch he would look, and by that time it would be next week.

Tee hee, ha ha, ho ho. This was hilarious. I mean, I could see and hear everything that was going on, and he had no idea that I was back there . . . ha ha ha . . . in the corner of the shed, virtually invisible to . . .

Slim was talking again. I clamped a lid on my laughter and listened.

"Hello, Stubtail. Are you happy to see old Slim? Well, you should be, 'cause I'm so wonderful. I'm happy to see you too, only you ain't the one I'm looking for."

This was great! He'd called *me* and had gotten Drover instead. Well, when he got tired of looking for me, maybe he would take Drover to school. Wouldn't that be a scream? One hour of Drover would be enough to wreck any school.

I choked down my laughter and strained to hear some more.

"Yes, you're a nice little doggie, and you know what? I'll give you a piece of my homemade beef jerky if you'll find Hank."

HUH?

The smile I had been wearing turned into a limp dishrag. Drover wouldn't do that . . . would he? Sell out a friend for one measly piece of beef jerky? I mean, Slim's jerky wasn't all that great to start with. I had almost choked on it several times. It was like chewing saddle leather. No, I was pretty sure that Drover would never . . .

They came inside the shed, Drover in the lead and Slim following. Drover stopped and looked back at Slim. Slim shook his head. "No, we're looking for Hank. I don't think he's in here."

Whew! Boy, there for a second . . .

WHAT?!

Drover barked and . . . you won't believe this . . . the little traitor turned and *pointed his nose straight at me*! I scrunched down and pressed myself into the chair, held my breath and listened.

A cunning smile slithered across Slim's mouth and he walked deeper into the shed. "Hmmmm. Now, I wouldn't have thought of looking in here. That would be pretty foxy, old Hank laying low in here." He walked up to Drover and stopped. "So you think he's back there in the shadows?"

I couldn't believe it. Drover barked again and pointed his cheating little nose straight at me. I pressed myself even deeper into the chair, ceased all breathing operations, and waited.

Slim pushed his hat to the back of his head and chewed on his lip. "Oh, I don't think he's here. Come on, let's look outside."

Whew! As they walked toward the door, I dared to grab a breath of air. That had been way too close for comfort, and I would definitely speak to Drover about this.

They stepped outside. Slim dug into his shirt pocket and pulled out . . . hmmm, it appeared to be a shriveled-up piece of beef jerky, but why would he . . .

He pitched the jerky into the air and Drover snapped it up. "Thanks, pooch, I appreciate the tip." Then Slim stepped back inside and . . . what? *Closed the sliding doors?*

Uh oh. All at once I was having bad feelings

about this. I mean, why would he . . . why would he be wearing that evil grin and why was he coming in my direction?

"Hi, puppy. I know you're in here."

That was a big fat lie. He didn't know I was in there. He couldn't have known. I was invisible in the Secret Sanctuary. Was he going to take the word of a little fraud like Drover? Drover couldn't even find himself half the time, much less find me. This was just a bluff, a fishing expedition in the dark.

"Nice doggie. Come to Slim."

Nice doggie, my foot. I'd heard that before.

He stopped, reached down, and picked up a piece of binder's twine off the floor. "Now, Hankie, you can either come out and surrender, or I'll go back there and root you out. If I have to root you out, I'm liable to get all dusty and dirty, and then I won't be my usual sweet self. What'll it be?"

What would it be? I cut my eyes from side to side and ran my options through Data Control. Things were looking bleak. This was a moment of truth. I decided to . . . RUN.

Yes, I would make a run for it. I had speed on my side, tremendous speed, awesome speed. I leaped out of the chair and made a dash to the south.

"Hank, come here! Stop!"

He could forget that. Right away, I encountered a few items of . . . clang, bang . . . junk lurking in the gloom: a coffee table, a box of photographs, and something tall and skinny that fell over with a crash. Okay, maybe it was a floor lamp, but floor lamps belong on the floor, right? So it was no big deal that it fell over, and it wasn't my fault.

I plowed my way through the junk and finally broke out into a clearing. I dashed straight to the place where the two sliding doors met, just in case Slim had been careless and had left enough of a crack for me to squirt through. No luck there.

He was coming after me. "Nice Hankie, come to Slim."

No, I was not going to be taken alive.

He was closing in on me. My gaze darted around the shed. Okay, I would have to blow a hole through one of the sliding doors. I hated to destroy their doors, but I had no choice. I grabbed a deep breath of air, squared my enormous shoulders, faced the door, and pushed the throttle lever all the way to Turbo Six. There was a deafening roar, an explosion of flames and smoke, and I went streaking toward the . . .

BONK.

. . . floor. In a heap. Ouch. Okay, the door turned out to be stouter than you might have supposed,

but that didn't stop me from . . . well, slithering under the workbench. Yes, I was aware that it wasn't a great place to hide, but I had run out of great places. The underside of the workbench would have to do until I could . . .

He came slouching toward me, twirling that piece of twine around his bony finger. "Hank, you can quit anytime now."

No.

I began creeping to the north. So did he. I reversed position and began creeping toward the south. So did he. I tried another northward creep. Again, he cut me off. Our eyes met.

"Give it up, pooch. Heck, we're going to send you to Doggie University."

Doggie University, ha! Did he think he was being funny? It was a School for Dumbbells, and I didn't need any of their so-called obedience training. I was as obedient as I needed to be, and just to prove it, I tried to make another dash to the south, but once again he blocked my path.

Okay, he had driven me to the wall and left me with one last option. I would have to go into the Jackhammer and Backhoe Program and dig my way through eight inches of solid concrete. Did you think that dogs can't do such things? Most can't and most won't even attempt it, but a few of us will do it when it's forced upon us. But I can tell you this: it sure messes up a barn floor.

I began flipping switches and went straight into the Jack-Back Program. (In times of stress, we shorten "Jackhammer and Backhoe Program" to "Jack-Back," don't you see. It saves time.) Anyway, I did the so-forth and suddenly the whole barn echoed with the brutal sounds of steel grinding away at rock.

SCRAPE. SCREEK. SLASH. GRIND. GROAN. SNAP.

It was an awful noise. Maybe you've seen heavy equipment tearing down huge buildings. Same deal. Sparks, smoke, dust, and the deafening rumble of solid steel making hash of solid concrete. It was . . .

HUH?

It was over, I mean, in the blink of an eye. He slipped the noose around my neck and gave it a jerk. "Let's go, pooch. We'll want to get you to bed early tonight so's you'll be fresh for school."

Oh. Okay, sure, no problem. School? Gee, that might be fun. I fell in step beside him, a loyal dog and his master, and together we made our way to the sliding doors. In front of the doors, we stopped. I rolled my eyeballs upward and gave my tail Slow Thoughtful Wags.

He looked down at me. "Now, I'm fixing to open the door, but don't get any big ideas."

Big ideas? I didn't know what he was talking about. I mean, he had to open the door so we could go outside, right?

He pushed the east door and it rumbled open. Outside, in front of my very eyes, I saw the wide-open spaces, and Freedom. Foolish man! Did he think I was going to sit there and watch the birds? I saw my opportunity and went lunging . . .

GULK.

Okay, twine. Did you forget that he had noosed me with a piece of baling twine? Ha ha. Sometimes we get so wrapped up in other things, we forget about those little details, don't we? Ha ha.

Anyway, we . . . uh . . . left the machine shed and headed toward Slim's pickup.

CHAPTER TEN

Slim Inflicts
a Song on Me

We had parked Slim's pickup down near the
gas tanks. Once again, I fell right in step
beside my master, marching to the drum of a distant beet. The beat of a distant drum, I guess it
would be, because beets are vegetables, similar to
turnips, and they don't play drums.

But the point is that I marched proudly beside
my master. I wanted the whole world to see and
know that . . . well, here was an *obedient* dog, a
dog who had learned manners and discipline, a
dog who wanted nothing more from life than to
please His People.

Was this the kind of dog you'd send off to a
cold, forbidding school, where they beat the dogs

three times a day with a wet noodle and sent them to bed, hungry and crying?

No sir. This was the kind of dog you'd want to keep at the ranch, at home, around a nice warm fire. You sure wouldn't want to send such an obedient friend off to some kind of awful school with . . . well, dungeons and torture chambers.

As we walked along, I peeked up at Slim to see if . . . well, if my New Dog Campaign was making an impression on him. I mean, there was still time for him to realize that he and Loper had acted in a moment of anger. They'd made a bad decision. They had completely misjudged my character. What we had here was just a little misunderstanding. No big deal, nothing major.

As we strolled past the gas tanks, I saw Drover on his gunnysack bed, but that wasn't the part that grabbed my attention. Right beside him, on MY gunnysack bed, was a cat. Pete. He raised his head, smirked, and waved his paw.

When Drover saw me, a look of horror passed over his face. "Hank, I didn't mean to do it, honest, but that jerky smelled so good . . ." And with that, he dived underneath his gunnysack.

We walked on. Would I find it in my heart to forgive the little tattletale? Heck no. At my first opportunity, I would give him the thrashing he so

richly deserved, and then I would give an even
better thrashing to the cat.

We reached the pickup and Slim opened the
door. "You ride in the cab, where I can keep an eye
on you."

I was shocked. Did he think I still had escape on
my mind? Fine, I would ride in the cab. I leaped up
on the seat and ran straight for the . . .

"It's rolled up."

. . . window. *What was wrong with him?* Every time I moved a muscle, he thought I was trying to escape! For his information, I had been merely checking to see . . . hey, we dogs like to hang our heads out of windows. We like fresh air, okay? What was the big deal?

He started the pickup and gave me a grin. "Hank, I can read you like a book. Every time you have a thought, which is about once every six months, it shows up like the lights of downtown Dallas."

Hmmm. I, uh, wasn't aware that my thoughts were so . . . I would have to be more careful. But that didn't give him the right to insult me and accuse me of terrible crimes. Dogs have feelings too.

We chugged away from ranch headquarters and Slim started humming a tune. Oh brother. Was this the beginning of another of his corny songs? Trapped inside the cab, would I have to endure another of his Crimes Against Music? I held my breath and waited. The humming went on, like the drone of a dozen wasps, but apparently he couldn't think of any words boring enough to match the tune, so I was spared.

Whew. You know, those songs of his really put

me in an awkward position. I mean, I like the guy and we've had some good times together, but those songs . . . see, he makes them up and sings them to us dogs! That's pretty weird, a grown man performing songs in a ranch pickup for his dogs, but he does it all the time.

And what can we do, what can we say? We don't want to be cruel and let him know that . . . well, that he has a lousy singing voice and writes songs that are incredibly dumb.

That would be cruel and insensitive, and furthermore, a dog could get fired for that kind of honesty. *They don't want to know what we really think.* All they want is praise and slavish devotion. We do the best we can, but sometimes it can be pretty embarrassing.

But this time the humming didn't develop into anything more serious and I wasn't forced to choose between my pride and my job. At the mailbox, we turned right on the county road and drove east toward Slim's shack, where I would be imprisoned for the night.

I stole a glance at Slim. Had he changed his mind about taking me to that ridiculous school? Had my New Dog Program softened his heart even a little bit? His face told me nothing. In other words, no. Unless something drastic happened between now and morning, he would haul me into town.

Up to this point, I had managed to keep up my courage, but things were beginning to look hopeless and a shiver of dread passed through my entire body. I had hoped that, through displays of Perfect Behavior, I could talk Slim out of it, but that had flopped.

Okay, maybe I'd been partly to blame. Viewed from a certain angle, you could say that my numerous attempts to escape might have been mistaken for . . . well, further proof that I had a problem with . . . obedience, shall we say. And since that was the whole issue, obedience, you might even argue that I had managed to dig myself even deeper into the hole of . . . something. Suspicion, I suppose.

Yes, Slim had grown very suspicious of me, almost as though he didn't . . . well, trust me. That's why he had noosed me with the twine and forced me to ride in a closed cab with the windows rolled up, right? In other words, even though I had tried and tried to present myself as a New Dog, a wiser, more mature dog, an obedient dog in every way . . .

Oh brother. How do these things happen?

I didn't know, but I was sure of one thing. The thought of going to that school *scared the liver out of me*. Are you shocked that a dog of my stature would be afraid? Sorry, I didn't want to admit it and I put it off as long as I could. You know how I am about the kids. I want them to think of me as courageous and bold, not as a quivering little weenie like Drover who's afraid of his own shadow.

So let's don't tell the little children that I had become a nervous wreck. Not only was I shivering all over, but I had started . . . well, chewing my foot. Why? I don't know, but that's what dogs do when we have an attack of nerves.

Slim's gaze drifted over to me. "What's wrong with you?"

How could he ask such a question? The cad.

"You ain't nervous about going to that school, are you?"

He was going to take me to a torture chamber tomorrow morning, so how was I supposed to feel? Of course I was nervous!

"Oh, quit worrying. It'll be fun."

Oh sure.

"You'll meet lots of new dogs."

Right, and the Dungeon Keeper who already hated my guts for snatching his wig. I could hardly wait.

We had been poking along the road at about ten miles an hour. Now we coasted over to the side of the road and stopped. "Would it help if I sang you a song?"

I stared at him in disbelief. NO!!

"Well, I'll sing you a good one if you'll beg."

Beg! Oh brother.

"In fact, I'll sing it even if you don't beg. You'll love this, pooch."

See? What did I tell you? I heaved a weary sigh and prepared my ears for the worst.

Hankie's Going to School

For years he's been a fool
But Hankie's going to school.
We just can't wait 'til he graduates
He'll come out more than cool.

In less than just a week
He'll learn to write and speak.
He'll be the rage, walk across the stage,
With fluency in Greek.

    He'll learn so many manners, he'll run
        off all his fleas,
      Saying, "Howdy do" and "How are you?"
        and "May I, pretty please?"

The mutt don't have much sense,
He's really pretty dense, but

He'll learn to catch and maybe fetch,
And learn obedience.

They'll teach him to obey,
We'll all be shocked and say,
"We're just agog, is that our dog?
Well, glory be, hurray!"

He'll be a model student, we can
    safely bet
He'll lead the class in etiquette
    and be the teacher's pet.

For college he is bound,
Our smelly dingbat hound,
We always thought he might have got
His schooling in the pound.

Old Hankie's been a mule
He's broken every rule,
But that's all past because he has
Enrolled in Manners School.

He gave me a broad grin and wiggled his eyebrows. For reasons unknown to me, he seemed very
proud of himself. "What do you think, Hankie?
Ain't that a cute little song? Tell me the truth."

I turned my back on him and stared out the window. The guy just didn't take hints. I had nothing to say. Well, I had plenty to say but it had all been said before, so what was the point? His song wasn't cute, my being sent to Dungeon School wasn't funny, and that was about the end of it.

Behind my back, he mumbled, "Dumb dog. You've got no more class than a bowl of pork and beans."

He slipped the gearshift up into first and started to pull out into the road again, but just then a pickup popped over a hill in front of us. For a moment it appeared that we would all be killed in a grinding head-on collision, but Slim jerked the wheel to the right and slammed on the brakes. It all happened so suddenly, I wasn't able to set up a bracing maneuver, and went flying into the dashboard.

As I picked myself off the floorboard and roasted Slim with an angry glare, he chuckled. "Oops, sorry, pooch."

If he was so sorry, why was he laughing about it? This time, maybe it had been an accident, but with these cowboys you never know. Sometimes they slam on the brakes and throw us out of our seats just because they have nothing more constructive to do. They don't seem to know or care that it's very embarrassing when the Head of Ranch Security rams his nose into the dashboard.

The pickup we had almost creamed pulled up right beside us and stopped. The lady driver rolled down her window and said, "Sorry, Slim, I didn't see you coming."

Slim's jaw dropped. So did mine. We both stared at the lady behind the wheel. She had the prettiest pair of blue eyes I'd ever seen and her hair was pulled back in a ponytail. Holy smokes, it was . . .

At last Slim found his voice. "Why, Miss Viola!" He realized that he was speaking into a rolled-up window, so he cranked down the glass. "Afternoon, Viola. No, it was my fault. Me and Hank were having a little argument. I sang him a wonderful song and he was too stubborn to clap and cheer."

She leaned her head back and laughed. "Honestly, Slim, you're the only man I know who sings to his dog."

"Well, I'm fixing to quit if he don't start showing more appreciation. Makes me feel like I'm wasting my talent."

She looked at us with her sparkling blue eyes. "You two are quite a pair." Then her gaze went past Slim and landed on me. "Hello, Hank."

For a moment, I forgot to breathe. A wave of warm feelings washed over my face. Have we discussed Miss Viola? She lived with her elderly parents on a ranch two or three miles below Slim's place, and some people whispered that she and Slim were sweet on each other. I knew the truth. She was actually sweet on ME and had to put up with Slim, just because the two of us ran around together.

And there she was, only two feet away from me! Maybe you think I just sat there looking simple and counting the flies on the wall. Ha. Not me, fellers. I did what any normal, intelligent, red-blooded American dog would have done. I climbed over Slim, launched myself out the window, and somehow managed to execute a perfect landing in Miss Viola's lap.

She gave a yelp of surprise and Slim growled, "Hank, for crying in the bucket!"

Well, what did he expect? He was too shy and awkward (and dumb) to show her the proper devotion, so that left the job for me. In other words, he'd just been shot out of the saddle. Viola and I were together at last. Now we could . . . well, run off and get married and live everly happy afterly.

Happily ever after, let us say. And besides, it had suddenly occurred to me that as long as I was sitting in her fond embrace, Slim couldn't send me off to Torture School. Viola would never allow that to happen.

I turned to her, looked deeply into her eyes, and beamed her a throbbing gaze that said, "Miss Viola, you would never allow cruel Slim to haul me off to a dungeon, would you?"

Maybe she didn't understand my urgent message, and before I could reload and try it again, Slim was already out of his pickup and trying to drag me out of her lap.

CHAPTER ELEVEN

A Date with Miss Viola

What did he expect me to do, just lie there like a mop and let him tear me out of the embrace of the woman who loved me so dearly? Heck no. I went to Full Lockdown and sank my claws into . . .

Well, her legs, for one thing, and I'll admit that wasn't the best thing to do. She kind of screeched, but it was a nice screech, not one that said, "Get out of my sight, you nasty dog!" It was more like, "Ouch, maybe you could be a little more gentle with your claws." Yes, it was a fond screech, actually more of a squeal than a screech.

Slim opened the door and dragged me out, then pitched me back into his pickup. "Doofus," he grumbled, then took a step toward Viola. He

102

stopped, groaned, and pushed a kink out of his back.

She noticed. "Did you hurt your back?"

"Oh, it's just a little catch. I need to go the the choirpractor one of these days. Sorry about Hank, ma'am, and I hope he didn't ruin your clothes."

"Oh, it's all right. Actually, it's kind of flattering." She smiled and fluttered her eyelids.

Slim didn't notice. "He's been acting weird ever since he found out I'm going to take him to Obedience School." He told her all about the day's . . . uh . . . dark events, shall we say. "Loper pitched a fit and now I have to . . ." He gazed up a the sky and shuffled his boots. "Say, Viola, how'd you like to go with me in the morning?"

"Is this . . . a date?"

"Well . . . sort of . . . I guess so . . . sure. You might have a calming effect on Birdbrain here and . . . well, I'd enjoy your company too."

She studied him for a long moment. "Slim, this isn't like you. It's so . . . romantic. Going on a date to an Obedience School for dogs!"

Slim's Adam's apple did flips and his face turned red. "Maybe it wasn't such a great idea. Just skip it."

She reached out a hand and touched his arm. "It's a wonderful idea and I'm so glad you thought of it. And yes, I'd be honored. I wouldn't miss it for the world."

Slim heaved a sigh and fanned his face with his hat. "I'll pick you up around eight-thirty."

She waved good-bye and drove away. Slim climbed back into the pickup and we started down the road again. He gave me a nullifying glare and didn't say another word. What was his problem? Hey, I had gotten him a date with the cutest, sweetest single lady in Ochiltree County, so what was he steamed about? Without my help, do you suppose he'd have had enough sense to ask her to a dance or a movie or some normal place where people go?

Heck no, but I got no thanks for it. Instead, he sulked and brooded all the way to the house. That was fine with me. I had nothing more to say to him, and he sure didn't have anything I wanted to hear, especially another corny song. I turned my back to him and we rode the rest of the way in stony silence.

It was almost dark by the time we walked into the house. Slim shuffled into the kitchen and started building himself a ketchup-and-canned-mackerel sandwich. I took a big yawn and stretch, rolled over on my back, and surrendered my weary bones to the . . .

I sat up and glanced around. Slim was busy in

the kitchen, right? Busy with other things and wasn't watching me, right? Heh heh. Foolish man. Did he think I'd forgotten about *tomorrow*? As quietly as a thief, I rose to my feet and began stalking around the outside walls, sniffing doors, windows, holes in the baseboard, searching for any tiny opening that might allow me to . . .

SNAP! A mousetrap?

Okay, whid your bind is focused on bustig out of brison, the last thig you'd ever expegg is to stigg your dose into one of Slibb's stubid *bousetrabs*. You talk about surbrised. That thig was cocked and loaded, and it put a derrible bide on the soft leathery end of by doze. Did it hurd? You bed it hurd!

Aaaaaa-oooooo!

I jumped three feet straight up, hopped around in circles, ran backward down the hall, and finally . . . uh . . . found myself standing in the kitchen. Slim was slouched against the refrigerator, gnawing on a folded piece of bread with ketchup oozing out the bottom. Our eyes met. This was very embarrassing and I switched my tail over to Slow Swings.

"Hank, give it up. You're going to school in the morning and you might as well get used to it."

Okay. I would quid tryigg to escabe if he would gedd the bousetrab off by doze. Honest. Doe kiddig.

He shoved the last of the sandwich into his mouth, licked the ketchup off his fingers, leaned over, and pried the trap off my nose. He straightened up, grunted something about the kink in his back, and said, "There. Now go to bed, and I don't want to hear any more out of you."

Yes sir. I lowered my head and tail into the Groveling Position and went slinking back to my spot in front of the stove. I collapsed on the floor and curled up into a ball. And for the rest of the night, I dreamed about dark dungeons and cackling villains. It was a terrible night and I hardly slept a wink.

Okay, I slept pretty well, but do you know how I did it? I counted goats.

Slim rousted me out of bed at eight-fifteen the next morning, nudging my tail section with the toe of his boot. "Wake up, sunshine, it's your first day of school. This time tomorrow, you'll have a college degree in Obedience."

Very funny.

I dragged myself off the miserable piece of fabric that passed for "carpet" in Slim's dump of a house and made my way to the front door. There, the man who had once been my friend placed the twine around my neck, and together we made the long, lonely walk to the pickup. I made no more attempts to escape. They had beaten me down and worn me out. Sometime in the night, I had resigned myself to my fate.

We pulled up in front of Miss Viola's house and she came skipping off the porch and down the sidewalk. My eyes popped open, my ears leaped up, and my tail began thrashing the seat. Holy smokes, she looked gorgeous! As fresh as the morning, as bright as a spring sky, and pretty as a field of wildflowers. She jumped into the cab and immediately changed its smell from . . . well, from dirty socks to rose pedals and cinnamon sticks, sugar and apple cider and . . . WOW!

Slim and I stared at her with open mouths. She gave us a puzzled smile. "Hi. Is anything wrong?"

Slim swallowed and stammered, "Good honk, Viola, you look prettier than three dips of ice cream."

She chirped a laugh. "Well, you look kind of dashing yourself. Is that a new shirt?"

"Sort of. I found it under my bed." He was so shook up, he turned the starter key, even though the motor was still running. It made a grinding screech. He threw the pickup into gear and off we went.

At that point, you probably think that I launched myself into Viola's lap. No sir. I held my position in the middle of the seat until we crossed the first cattle guard on the way to town. Only then did I begin easing myself in her direction, creeping inch by inch until I could feel her warm shoulder next to mine. Then, in a very casual manner, I lifted my right front paw and placed it on her lap. Moments later, I eased my head onto her leg and wiggled forward until my left front paw joined the right one. She started rubbing me behind the ears and stroked me under the chin and . . .

Gee, it was so nice being close to her, I forgot all about the Dungeon of Doom and why we were going into town. I closed my eyes and listened to the hum of the motor and forgot all my troubles, and the next thing I knew . . .

The pickup slowed to a stop. We were already in town. I sat up and glanced around, expecting to see a huge stone castle with buzzards circling above it, and Rudy the Dungeon Keeper snapping his whip, and a bunch of naughty little mutts begging their masters to take them home.

But that's not what I saw. In front of me was a broad field of green grass and trees, shrubs and pretty flowers. We had come to City Park, of all places, and it appeared that someone was having a picnic. There were maybe twenty cars parked along the curb, and out in the wide grassy area I saw a crowd of people with dogs on leashes. The people were chatting and laughing, and in the middle of it all stood Rudy Teacher, looking pleasant and charming and . . . well, kind of normal.

I shot a glance at Slim. This was Obedience School? Why hadn't he told me it would be a picnic in the park? I mean, I had spent the past twenty-four hours worrying myself sick and preparing for some kind of . . .

Okay, you thought they were sending me to some kind of awful experience in a dungeon, right? Ha ha. And maybe for a little while I'd thought so too, but sometimes our imaginations run wild, see, and we worry about . . . well, silly things.

I took a deep breath of fresh air. You know, maybe this school wasn't going to be so bad after all.

Slim and Viola got out of the pickup. Slim said, "Come on, Hankie, let's go meet your classmates."

Classmates. Gee, that had a nice sound to it. I crept across the seat, looked around in all directions, and hopped down. Slim gave the leash a tug and the three of us strolled over to the crowd. I was breathing easier now. You know, it's funny, all the crazy things a guy imagines when he's facing a situation that's new and different. Ha ha. Dungeon

Keepers. Torches on the walls. Torture chambers. Ha ha.

We melted into the crowd and Viola struck up a conversation right away. She introduced Slim to someone and all at once they were chatting. And get this. Rudy saw us and came over to say hello, and to my complete amazement, he told Viola the story about how I had . . . uh . . . you know, the Dead Squirrel Incident. The day before, he'd been ready to throw me out of school, but now he told it as a funny story on himself.

He even rubbed me on the head and said, "That was a good one, Hank. It just took me a while to laugh about it."

Well, that took a big load off my mind. I mean, you don't want to start school when the teacher already hates you. This deal was looking better and better, and all at once I felt a rush of new confidence. Going to Dog School just might turn out to be a lot of fun, and I just might turn out to be the Star Student.

Why not? I mean, consider my long list of skills and qualifications: experience running a big ranch and serving as Head of the Security Division; charm, wit, intelligence, patience, good manners, and the kind of dashing good looks that always made a big impression on the lady dogs.

Someone had to finish at the top of the class, right? I figured it might as well be me.

I glanced around at my new classmates. A cute little Pomeranian gal sat nearby, so I turned to her and gave her a wolfish smile.

"Hank the Cowdog, Head of Ranch Security. Big day, huh? What's your name, sugar pie?"

She looked me over and curled her lip. "Alexandria. Where did they find *you*, at the city dump?" Then she turned to a dog next to her and whispered, "I was afraid of this. They're letting in riffraff!"

CHAPTER TWELVE

Not a Perfect Ending, but Close Enough

Huh? Riffraff!

I ran my gaze over the crowd of dogs and suddenly realized that ... gulp ... they were all *house dogs*, and we're talking about bathed and brushed and blow-dried, sparkling and perfumed and wearing little ribbons in their hair.

There wasn't a ranch dog or a cowdog in sight, not even a bird dog!

All at once my mouth seemed very dry and I noticed a tightness in my throat. I edged away from the snooty Pomeranian and moved closer to Viola's legs.

Just then, Rudy clapped his hands together

and called for silence. "Folks, I think we're all here. Welcome to Rudy's Obedience School! We're going to have a lot of fun today, so let's get started with a little routine we call Walking Fido." He laughed at his own humor. "I want each of you to walk your little friend back and forth in front of the class so that we can get an idea of where we are in the training process."

He pointed to a lady in the crowd. "We'll start with Mrs. Bisby and her adorable little Pomeranian, Alexandria. I think you'll be impressed, folks."

I happened to glimpse Alexandria when her name was called. She looked at me down the end of her nose and sniffed, "Watch this, clodhopper."

She and her lady stepped forward and prissed back and forth in front of the crowd. Alexandria never missed a cue, never got out of step. The audience loved it and clapped their approval.

I was getting a bad feeling about this. Hey, if the little snoot was so perfect, what was she doing here? Some of us had never done "Walking Fido" in front of a bunch of people and might have a little trouble . . . had all these dogs done this before?

Two more dogs and their owners made the walk. Perfect. Not a hitch.

I began to feel the pressure. What if a guy missed a step or stumbled or suddenly got drilled

114

by a flea? Did those other dogs even *have* fleas? I did, and that tightness in my throat got worse and my legs were starting to shake.

Rudy's eyes prowled the crowd and stopped on . . . gulp . . . Slim. "Mr. Chance! Show us what a working ranch dog can do."

Oh no! I tried to hide.

Slim sucked in a big breath of air. "Well, we're on, pooch."

I can't explain this. I don't know how or why it happened, but all at once my legs just . . . turned to jelly. I sank to the ground. I felt that I was choking. I couldn't breathe or move.

Slim pulled on the leash. "Come on, Hank, don't quit me now."

He didn't understand. This was no joke. I had actually been stricken with some kind of terrible paralyzing disease—Leg Jelliosis. It struck without warning and there was no cure for it. No kidding.

His eyes came at me like bullets. "Hank, will you get up?" From somewhere in the crowd, I heard a snicker of laughter. Slim's eyeballs seemed to be bulging out of his head. "Hank, if you don't get your carcass off that ground . . ."

I didn't hear the rest of his message. It was buried under a wave of laughter. I was paralyzed,

Slim was ready to skin me alive, and THEY WERE LAUGHING AT US.

Slim's face turned a deep shade of red. He looked at Rudy. "Y'all go on with your school. I'm taking this bozo back to the ranch. Sorry for the inconvenience."

There was another ripple of chortles and chuckles. Everyone was watching us. I caught a glimpse of Alexandria. She was whispering to a little cocker spaniel and they both squealed with laughter.

Slim towered over me, shaking his head and moving his lips. Hey, did he think I'd planned all of this? Did he think I was having fun?

He hitched up his jeans, bent over, grabbed me around the middle, and hoisted me off the ground. Muttering under his breath, he started toward the pickup. He took five steps and . . . well, I noticed that his back was still bent at an angle. That seemed odd. Then he stopped and dropped me like a load of laundry.

"Viola," he said in a low voice, "my back just went out on me."

What? Of all the times for his back to go out! I glanced around at the crowd. People were watching and whispering behind their hands. I had never been so embarrassed. Right there in front of half the town of Twitchell . . . oh brother!

Miss Viola stepped up and took hold of my leash. Maybe it was her warm presence that cured my Leg Jelliosis, or maybe we'll never know, but strength returned to my withered legs and we walked together, side by side, to the pickup—a loyal dog and the lady who loved him.

You know, I think I could have done Walking Fido with her. Heck, I could have walked ten thousand miles over hot coals with Miss Viola. Too bad Slim didn't think of that.

He followed along behind, muttering and walking like . . . something. A turkey. A crab. An old man bent in half at the middle. He looked pretty stove up. And mad, very mad.

Viola helped Mr. Grump into the bed of the pickup. He stretched out in the back and told her to drive him straight to the chiropractor. By this time, all the pressure of my schooling had vanished and I felt great, so I hopped up into the cab and rode through town with the prettiest gal in Ochiltree County. No bad deal, huh?

As we made our way toward Dr. Whitehead's office on the south edge of town, Viola smiled to herself, then started laughing so hard that she almost ran off the road. "I'll swear, when you go on a date with Slim Chance, you never know what you'll be doing. I know he's hurting, poor man, but honestly, this is the funniest thing I ever heard of!"

I agreed. When he wasn't trying to be funny, Slim could be hilarious.

We pulled up in front of the chiropractor's office and Viola helped the invalid inside. Dr. Whitehead spent half an hour putting Slim's bones back where they were supposed to be, and Slim came out looking better. He wasn't walking like a turkey anymore and he felt good enough to ride in the cab with me and my lady fair—much to my disappointment.

Viola drove us back to the ranch. The air inside the cab was so heavy and dark, you'd have thought someone was burning tires. I was afraid to move. Slim sat slumped against the door and didn't say a word. Miss Viola kept her eyes on the road and was as solemn as a statue.

We pulled up in front of Slim's shack and Viola shut off the motor. Silence. Nobody knew what to say. Then Slim growled, "Your daddy'll love this story."

Viola tried to hold back her laughter but it came spilling out. A smile twitched at the corners of Slim's mouth, then he started laughing too. I sat between them, unsure of, uh, how to respond. I mean, a guy could lose his job . . .

Viola helped him into the house, pulled off his

boots, and helped him lie down on the bed. She left a stack of books and magazines beside his bed, and brought him a glass of water.

He thanked her and said, "Just drive my pickup home, Viola. I won't be needing it for a few days."

"I'll check on you this evening and bring you some supper."

He nodded and turned his eyes up to the ceiling. "Viola, if I'd had any idea . . ."

She brought a finger to her lips. "Shhh. I needed to get out of the house anyway, and it was . . . it was an experience to remember."

Slim let out a groan. "It derned sure was."

They shared a laugh and she went on home.

As you might expect, I found it convenient to . . . uh . . . stay as far away from Slim as I possibly could. I mean, our relationship had definitely hit bottom, so I curled up in the northwest corner of the living room and tried to sleep. Minutes passed, maybe an hour. Then I heard his voice calling from the back of the house.

"Hank? Come here." Gulp. I had been summoned. With great misgivings, I crept through the house and stood beside his bed. "Come here. I ain't going to bite." I moved closer. His bony hand reached out and . . . whew . . . began scratching behind my ears. I almost fainted with relief. "Hank,

120

I appreciate your help in ruining my social life. I ain't sure I could have done it on my own."

Gee, it was nice of him to say that.

"We make a pretty good team. I mess up my half and you mess up the rest."

Yes, we did make a pretty good team, come to think of it.

"I'll never be able to show my face in town again, but heck, I didn't want to go to town in the first place. Thanks for all the great memories."

We looked into each other's eyes. It was a touching moment and I felt kind of choked up with emotion.

"Now, go fetch my sheepskin slippers out of the living room. I may need to powder my nose here directly."

I sprang to my feet and went to Wild Swings on the tail section. Oh happy day, we were friends again! Could I fetch his slippers? You bet I could, and I didn't need a diploma from Obedience School to do it.

I rushed back into the living room and had no trouble locating the slippers. I picked one up in my jaws and . . . sniff, sniff . . . you know, sheepskin is pretty interesting material.

"Hank?"

It smells just like sheep, don't you see, and we

dogs very seldom get an opportunity to . . . well, study articles made of . . .

"Hank!"

You think I chewed up his slippers, don't you? Heh heh. No sir, didn't even think about it. Okay, I thought about it, but not for long. I resisted Temptation, delivered his slippers one by one, and received our ranch's Highest Award for Obedience.

And that's about all the story. Everything turned out fine. Slim recovered and never again threatened to send me to school, and Miss Viola . . . well, she fell even more deeply in love with me than before. Pretty amazing, huh? You bet.

Case closed.

Oh, remember all those nutty things we said about . . . you know, the Dungeon of Doom? I was misquoted, see, and don't forget that I'd been under a terrible emotional strain and . . .

Just forget 'em, okay? Thanks.

The following activities are samples from *The Hank Times*, the official newspaper of Hank's Security Force. Do not write on these pages unless this is your book. Even then, why not just find a scrap of paper?

"Photogenic" Memory Quiz

We all know that Hank has a "photogenic" memory—being aware of your surroundings is an important quality for a Head of Ranch Security. Now you can test your powers of observation.

How good is your memory? Look at the illustration on page 61 and try to remember as many things about it as possible. Then turn back to this page and see how many questions you can answer.

1. Which one of Hank's feet was stuck in a paint can?

2. What shelf were the jars on—the top, the middle, or the bottom?

3. Was the broomstick in front of the chair or under it?

4. Was the canoe upside-down or right side up?

5. Was Drover sitting on a chair or a couch?

6. How many of Hank's ears were pointing up—1, 2, or 3?

Decode Rip and Snort's Secret Message

U se the Coyote Code below to unscramble the following message intercepted at ranch headquarters.

	1	2	3	4	5	6
A	J	N	T	I	G	L
B	R	O	Y	S	U	C
C	W	A	M	H	G	E

"

C1 C6   B4 A4 A2 A5   C3 C6   A1 B5 B4 A3   C2

C1 B2 B1 A3 C4 A6 C6 B4 B4

!"

B6 B2 B3 B2 A3 C6

Hank's PicWords

Hank and his friends made some PicWords that need to be unscrambled. Use the character name or item illustrated below. Then subtract the letters indicated from each name or word. Add what's left over together and the PicWord will be solved. Good luck!

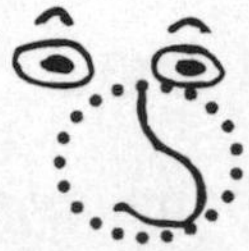

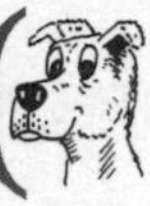

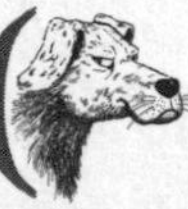

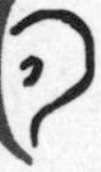

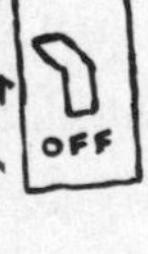

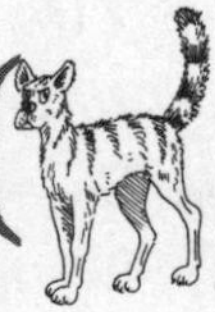

$$\left(\widehat{\text{☺}} - se \right) + \left(\text{🐕} - pe \right) =$$

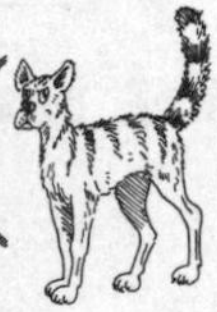

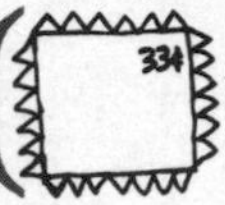

$$\left(\boxed{334} - amp \right) + \left(\text{🐕} - drr \right) =$$

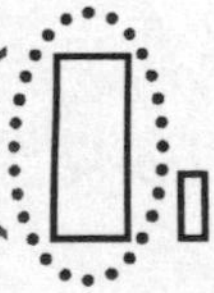

$$\left(\text{▯} - ig \right) + \left(\text{🐕} - h \right) + \left(\text{,} - a \right) =$$

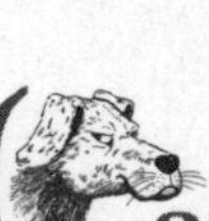

$$\left(\text{🐕} - ank \right) + \left(\text{OFF} - n \right) + \left(\text{🐕} - te \right) =$$

Have you read all
of Hank's adventures?

□ Yes, I want to join Hank's
Security Force. Enclosed
is $12.95 ($8.95 + $4.00
for shipping and handling)
for my **two-year member-
ship**. [Make check payable
to Maverick Books.]

**Which book would you like to receive in your
Welcome Package? Choose any book in the series.**

(#   )   (#   )
_____
FIRST CHOICE   SECOND CHOICE

                                    BOY or GIRL
_____
YOUR NAME   (CIRCLE ONE)

_____
MAILING ADDRESS

_____
CITY   STATE   ZIP

_____
TELEPHONE   BIRTH DATE

_____
E-MAIL

Are you a □ Teacher or □ Librarian?

Send check or money order for $12.95 to:

Hank's Security Force
Maverick Books
P.O. Box 549
Perryton, Texas 79070

DO NOT SEND CASH. NO CREDIT CARDS ACCEPTED.
Allow 4–6 weeks for delivery.

The Hank the Cowdog Security Force, the Welcome Package, and The
Hank Times _are the sole responsibility of Maverick Books. They are not
organized, sponsored, or endorsed by Penguin Group (USA) Inc., Puffin
Books, Viking Children's Books, or their subsidiaries or affiliates._